"Please don't quit, Piper. I know you need the job, and, more importantly, I know you want the job."

Just the thought of leaving made her want to weep, but it was for the best—wasn't it?

"We're adults," Max said. "Can't we find a way for this to work?"

Piper clasped her hands on her lap, but didn't respond right away.

Max took a deep breath. "I've thought about what I would say to you when, or if, I ever had the chance."

"You don't need to say anything." She shook her head, not wanting to discuss the past—at least, not now, not when she was still reeling from his sudden appearance in her life.

"I made a lot of mistakes, Piper, and I have a lot of regrets, but when I look back at my life, the biggest regret I have is how I treated you."

She didn't want to hear what he had to say, but she couldn't walk away now. There was a part of her that didn't ~~~~~~~~~~~~~~~~~~~rayal had wounded ~~~~~~~~~~~~~~~~logy didn't feel like e~~~~~~~~~~~~~~~~he offer?

Gabrielle Meyer lives in central Minnesota on the banks of the Mississippi River with her husband and four young children. As an employee of the Minnesota Historical Society, she fell in love with the rich history of her state and enjoys writing fictional stories inspired by real people and events. Gabrielle can be found at www.gabriellemeyer.com, where she writes about her passion for history, Minnesota and her faith.

Books by Gabrielle Meyer

Love Inspired

A Mother's Secret
Unexpected Christmas Joy
A Home for Her Baby

Love Inspired Historical

A Mother in the Making
A Family Arrangement
Inherited: Unexpected Family
The Gift of Twins

Visit the Author Profile page at Harlequin.com.

A Home for Her Baby

Gabrielle Meyer

LOVE INSPIRED
INSPIRATIONAL ROMANCE

LOVE INSPIRED®
INSPIRATIONAL ROMANCE

ISBN-13: 978-1-335-48869-5

A Home for Her Baby

This edition published by arrangement with Harlequin Books S.A.

For questions and comments about the quality of this book, please contact us at CustomerService@Harlequin.com.

Love Inspired
22 Adelaide St. West, 40th Floor
Toronto, Ontario M5H 4E3, Canada
www.Harlequin.com

Printed in U.S.A.

And above all things have fervent charity
among yourselves: for charity shall
cover the multitude of sins.
—*1 Peter* 4:8

To my daughter, Maryn.
I'm always amazed by your thoughtfulness,
mad organizational skills and your ability
to confidently rise to any challenge.
I love you, Maisy-May.

Chapter One

Max Evans stepped out of his Lexus and stared up at the large Warren House Bed & Breakfast. When he left Timber Falls ten years ago, he never imagined he'd be back. The truth was, he had hoped he wouldn't have to return. At least, not this soon. Coming back meant he'd failed, and failure was not an option. At least not for an Evans man. But Max didn't like who he'd become, and it was easy to pinpoint when it all started to go wrong. Maybe, by coming back to where he took a wrong turn, he could backtrack and make a better choice this time.

As long as he didn't choose to run again. Sometimes, it was easier to walk away than face failure.

The day was hot for the beginning of September and he had been driving for two days from Buffalo, New York. All he wanted was a shower and a place to crash inside the air-conditioned house—though he wasn't sure it would be quite so easy. There were still a lot of details he needed to oversee before he could sleep.

He went to the back of his Lexus and took out his large suitcase. He'd leave the rest inside the trunk and deal with it later.

"Max Evans?" a boy asked from a neighboring yard. He and his friends were tossing a football, but all of them stopped to stare at Max.

"Whoa!" said another. "You *are* Max Evans!"

Max smiled, but didn't encourage the boys to come over to say hi. He'd have to get used to the attention being back in his hometown, but right now, he needed some rest.

"Is it true you quit?" asked a third boy. "If I was in the NFL, I wouldn't quit."

Max didn't want to engage them, but he couldn't ignore them, either. "I retired," he said.

After playing in the NFL for six years, he'd been traded four times and suffered two serious injuries. The last one had been a concussion, shortly followed by talk of another trade. Max decided to retire before he was dropped, or before he had another injury.

"Are you staying there?" asked the first boy, pointing at the bed-and-breakfast.

Max glanced up at the massive house again and let the truth sink in. "I own this place."

"You're my neighbor?" asked the second boy. "Whoa!" he said again. "I'm gonna tell my mom." The boys took off toward the house, calling out to the boy's mom as they ran.

Max wondered if he knew who she was. Would she be happy to know Max was next door? Or would she forbid her son from talking to him? He didn't usually care what the public thought about him, but it was different in Timber Falls, Minnesota. Here, his friends and neighbors were more like family. And he'd always cared what his family thought about him. It had almost destroyed him when he messed up and disappointed his dad—and the whole town—ten years ago the night before the championship game. If he could go back, he would have said no to the college party, the alcohol and especially the girl.

He owed the town a state football championship title, which was the reason he'd chosen to finally return. The high school team needed a head football coach and with his recent retirement, he had all the time in the world. The school agreed to keep the news of his coaching job a secret until his arrival to prevent undue attention on the student players. Max didn't want them to have to deal with the publicity before he could be there to shoulder the burden for them.

The boys from next door were still loud enough to hear as Max walked up the sidewalk toward the house, a smile on his face. The whole neighborhood was like a page out of a Norman Rockwell calendar. Mature trees stretched over Third Street, their branches intertwining with the ones across the road. Up and down the street, Victorian-era homes graced the historic neighborhood. Each was painted in unique colors, boasting large windows, turrets and wraparound porches. But it was the Warren House that was the crown jewel, though it hadn't always been this pretty. Max remembered the house from his childhood. It had been run-down and abandoned for as long as he could remember. He had ridden his bike past it almost every day on the way to Piper Pierson's house.

Just thinking about Piper made the smile disappear from Max's face. She had been the one person in the world who knew him better than he knew himself, and the girl he thought he'd marry.

Now she was the woman who probably despised him more than any other. In a town as small as Timber Falls, it would be impossible to avoid her. The likelihood of seeing her again was the one thing that had made Max hesitate to return. He'd hurt her more than anyone else that fateful night and she'd be the hardest person to face.

But he couldn't run away forever; at least, that's what he kept telling himself. It was the only way to convince himself to come back to town.

An older woman appeared at the window in the heavy front door. She waved and smiled as she turned the knob to open it for him.

"Hello, Max!" Mrs. Roberta Anderson wore a floral apron tied around her waist. The middle-aged woman had a few careworn wrinkles at the corners of her twinkling eyes, but that was the only difference in her appearance.

"Mrs. Anderson." Max grinned, happy to see a familiar face. "I didn't expect you to be here."

"Didn't your mother tell you? I was hired to cook for the bed-and-breakfast."

"I didn't know, but I'm happy you're here." On the outside, he smiled, but inside, he was cringing. What had he been thinking when he bought this rambling old house? The first time his mother suggested it, he'd laughed at the idea, but then she told him the owner was a desperate widow who needed to sell. How could he say no? He had wanted to redeem the mistakes of his past and show Timber Falls he was truly sorry. What better way to invest in a business, *and* help an old widow? Besides, as the new head coach of the high school football team, he needed a place to stay—at least for this first season. The bed-and-breakfast had a third-floor apartment where he would live.

Max walked up the steps to the immense porch and received a hug from one of his mother's dearest friends.

"I can't believe she didn't tell you," Mrs. Anderson said.

"My mom took care of all the details." He winked at her. "I just signed the check."

She laughed and then stepped back to get a good look at him. "With my Henry gone, I needed to find a way to support myself." Her eyes became serious behind her glasses. "If it hadn't been for you, young man, I wouldn't have this job, so I can't thank you enough. It came at the perfect time."

"Don't thank me." Max wasn't comfortable taking credit where credit wasn't due. If his mother hadn't persisted, he wouldn't have bought the bed-and-breakfast. "My mom should get the praise." After the season was over, he'd have to make a more permanent decision. Maybe he'd sell the bed-and-breakfast and move on. Maybe he'd stay. He wasn't sure.

She opened the door wider. "It looks like you need some meat on your bones. Since I'm living in the apartment on the main floor, you can expect a hot breakfast, lunch and dinner every day."

"I wouldn't dream of asking you to cook for me." Max stepped into the elegant entry hall and closed the oak door behind him. The cooler air was tinged with the smell of lemon polish, old house and fresh flowers. A vase of late-summer daisies stood on a narrow table to his left.

"The bed-and-breakfast opens for business tomorrow," Mrs. Anderson said as they passed from the entry hall into the spacious foyer. "I'll be cooking for the guests. It won't be any trouble to cook for you, too."

"The house isn't open for business yet?"

"The final renovations happened last week. Tomorrow's the grand opening. We're finishing up all the last-minute details now."

Tomorrow was also the first day he'd start coaching the Timber Falls High School team. They had already been practicing for a couple weeks, though Max hadn't been able to come any sooner. He'd be there for their first away game tomorrow evening. It would be strange to return to the high school field after all these years.

"Is there anything I can do to help?" Max asked Mrs. Anderson. "I don't know how to run a bed-and-breakfast, but I'm willing to learn."

"You don't need to do a thing," she said. "That's why you have a staff."

It was the one stipulation he'd given his mother when she suggested he buy the place. He didn't want to deal with the day-to-day operations. All he knew was football—not hospitality. She said she'd take care of hiring a general manager and a cook and, apparently, she had.

"If there's anything I can do," he said, genuinely wanting to help if he could, "just let me know."

"You'll want to get settled in your apartment." Mrs. Anderson pointed to the grand staircase. The wood railing gleamed in the sunshine spilling through the lead glass windows. An elegant floral carpet runner covered the steps and accented the painted walls. "There's a set of steps in the middle of the second-floor hallway that lead to the third—" A timer rang somewhere deep within the house. "I hope you don't mind finding it on your own," she said, "but I have a pan of cookies I need to get out of the oven."

Before he could answer, she was gone.

Max stood in the foyer, the opulent home spreading out before him in every direction. It was almost too much to believe that he owned the house.

He started up the first flight of stairs, turning right at the landing, and then came to a long hall with nine or ten doors. One of the doors on the left opened and someone stepped out with a pile of white towels stacked high, covering her face. The first thing Max noticed was the tiny bump at her waist, indicating a pregnancy. She wasn't a tall woman. She was actually quite dainty, and the pile of towels towered over her head. Was this the general manager his mother had hired? Why would she hire someone who was expecting a baby? It couldn't be easy to run a bed-and-breakfast, even for the heartiest person.

The lady wore a white T-shirt and a pair of denim overalls, rolled up at the ankles. On her feet she wore white Converse shoes. She was clearly unaware of his presence as she stopped at another door, balancing the towels in one hand, while turning the doorknob with the other.

The towels wobbled and Max dropped his suitcase to rush to her side. He grabbed the towels before they toppled out of her hands.

"Here," he said as he placed his hands on the top and bottom of the pile, covering one of her hands. "Let me help."

She yelped in surprise and peeked out from behind the stack. Her large, violet-colored eyes opened wide.

At the same moment, Max's heart started to pound and his breath caught. "Piper."

She swallowed. "Max. Wh-what are you doing here?"

He hadn't seen her since his dad's funeral—and even then, he'd only seen her from across the church. They hadn't talked since that horrible night over ten years ago when she had found out he'd been kissing another girl—one he couldn't even name. It was the worst night of his life.

"I own this place." He took the towels from her hands. "What are you doing here?"

Piper's eyes grew even wider. She wore her long dark hair in a messy bun and had a smudge of dirt on her cheek—but he'd never seen anyone as pretty as his childhood girlfriend. The passage of time had been kind to her, and she was more beautiful than ever. "You bought—?" She didn't finish, the look of incredulity tilting her eyebrows together. "I had no idea. Your mom said the owner wanted to remain anonymous." She let out a sigh as her shoulders drooped. "I should have known."

"How could you?" Max set the towels on a hall table and kept one hand on the top to steady them. "For some reason, she thought it best if both parties were anonymous. I have no idea who the old widow is, either."

"Old widow?" Confusion marred Piper's pretty face.

"The old widow who sold me the house. My mother said she was in a desperate situation."

Piper groaned and started to turn away from him. "How could this happen?"

"I'm sorry." He wasn't quite sure what he was apologizing for, but if he knew anything, he knew he couldn't say it enough. "Did my mother hire you and not tell you who you'd be working for?"

"No—not really." She looked back at him, distrust and uncertainty in her face. "She didn't hire me. I'm the 'desperate old widow' you bought the house from."

"What?" Piper was a widow? Shock and disbelief gripped him. She'd married one of his good friends, Nick Connelly, around the same time Max's dad died. "Nick?"

She pressed her lips together and nodded, grief radiating from her eyes. "He died in a construction accident four months ago."

"Piper—" He took a step closer to her on instinct, but refrained from touching her. "I had no idea. No one told me. I wish I had known."

"If you had, what could you have done? It all happened so fast. There was nothing any of us could do."

Besides Piper, Nick had been Max's best friend all throughout school. Though it had almost destroyed Max when he heard Nick and Piper had gotten married, he hadn't been entirely surprised. After Max left, they had probably turned to each other naturally.

He didn't know what to say, so he said the first thing that came to mind. "I'm sorry for your loss, Piper. Nick was a good guy."

Something flashed in her eyes, but she covered it quickly. "He wasn't perfect, but he loved me." She lifted her chin, the stubborn spark in her eyes returning like an old friend he hadn't seen in years. If anyone could pick up the pieces of a broken life, it would be Piper.

"I'm sure he did love you," Max said gently. Who wouldn't love Piper?

She crossed her arms. "I suppose if you had known

I was the owner, you probably wouldn't have agreed to let me stay on and manage the bed-and-breakfast." She pointed to the back of the house. "I'll pack my things and be gone by tomorrow—"

"No." It was the last thing he wanted. How could he tell a pregnant widow she had to give up her job and move? Especially when it was Piper? "Stay, please. We'll figure something out."

Doubt passed over her face. He didn't blame her for not trusting him.

Max Evans had returned to Timber Falls. So many emotions mingled in Piper's heart, she could hardly focus on any of them. Anger. Heartbreak. Disappointment.

Hope.

She swallowed as she stared at the only man she had ever completely trusted—and the one who had hurt her deeper than any other. Why would she feel hopeful seeing Max again? He had abandoned all of them ten years ago with a chip on his shoulder. Had he come home to rub their faces in his success?

Despite her uncertainty, frustration mounted. "I'm confused," she said as she continued to cross her arms. The hallway was wide and long, but it felt as if the papered walls were closing in on Piper. She wished she was still holding the towels; at least then she wouldn't feel so exposed or vulnerable in front of her onetime hero. "Why are you back? Shouldn't you be at some training camp somewhere about now? Who was the last team you were playing for? The Buffalo Bills?"

His eyes were the brownest eyes she'd ever seen. Dark and full of so much depth, she used to get lost looking in them. Now, they were filled with regret and sadness. It hurt to look at him. She didn't want to feel sorry for him. He had hurt her—had hurt the entire town—he didn't deserve her compassion.

"I retired from the NFL and came back to coach the Timber Falls High School football team."

Piper's mouth slid open in surprise. "What?" She shook her head. "Aren't you in the prime of life? You have years left to play." The NFL had been his dream since he was little. It was the first thing he said to her when they met at Vacation Bible School as nine-year-olds.

It was Max's turn to look exposed and vulnerable as he shifted his weight and didn't meet her eyes. "It seemed like a good time to retire. I was ready to do something different and my mom told me that the Timber Falls Lumberjacks needed me."

She squinted her eyes as she regarded him. It wasn't as simple as that, she was certain. The way his mouth tightened and the way he held his shoulders told her a different story. He could never hide his real feelings from her, and now was no exception.

"You know I don't like when people hide things from me." She cocked an eyebrow, challenging him to deny her statement. "What really happened, Max?" He didn't owe her any explanation, and she probably didn't have a right to ask, but old habits were hard to break and they had never kept anything from each other. It had been the hallmark of their relationship: complete and honest truth, even when it was hard. It was the only way she had ever agreed to be friends with him in the first place—and the reason she'd eventually agreed to date him in high school.

"Do you need help with these towels?" he asked. "Mrs. Anderson said you have a lot to do before the grand opening. I don't want to keep you from getting it done." He lifted the towels and nodded toward the door she'd opened. "In here?"

"You can't avoid answering me, Max Evans. You know I'll eventually get the truth out of you." She always had.

He walked into the Garnet Room and stopped for a moment to look around. The walls were painted a rich dark yellow and the thick trim was stained a deep walnut which matched the headboard and footboard of the sleigh bed. A beautiful merlot-color bedspread brought out the shades of red in the stained glass at the top of the bay window. "This looks amazing, Piper." He shook his head in wonder. "Every time I rode by this place growing up, I had no idea how beautiful it would be inside." He studied her, his gaze briefly flicking to her stomach before he met her eyes again. "But you knew it would be beautiful, didn't you?"

It was true. Just like Max had always wanted to see the world and play professional football, Piper had known she wanted to stay in Timber Falls and buy the old Warren House to return it to its former glory. As a child, she had no idea what kind of a toll it would take on her marriage or her finances. Now that she knew, there was a part of her that wondered if she would have done things differently. Were her dreams worth so much pain?

But none of it mattered anymore. Nick had died, leaving her to pay off the immense debt they'd taken on—and the debt she didn't know he had created on the side. She'd often wondered why he wanted to hunt and fish every weekend he got the chance, but she'd thought it was because of their rocky relationship. After his accident, she realized he wasn't hunting or fishing. He was at the casino in a nearby town, feeding an addiction she didn't know he had until it was too late.

He'd kept the truth from her to try to protect her, but it had done the opposite. If she had known, maybe she could have helped.

He was simply one more person, in a long line of people, who had lied to her and broken her heart.

"You can put the towels in there." She pointed to the elegant bathroom beyond a thick walnut door.

Max did as she asked and set the towels on the shelf. When he came back into the bedroom, his gaze returned to her stomach and he asked softly, "Is this your first baby?"

Piper rested her hand on her growing midsection. The baby had been active all morning, but was now still. "Yes," she said just as gently.

Something akin to regret passed over Max's handsome face. "I'm sorry Nick won't be here to meet his child."

She was, too. It had taken them years to finally conceive after getting help from a fertility clinic. It meant spending more money, but Piper had wanted to be a mother more than anything else in life. She was torn between excitement and guilt. If it had been up to Nick, they would have never sought the help of a doctor. The cost of the procedures, and the mounting debt, had only increased his stress and put more strain on their relationship. She was almost certain he'd begun to gamble to pay off the bills—but it had only added to the trouble.

"I was a month along when he died," she said. "At least he knew we were finally expecting." It was a small comfort, especially when the pregnancy had made Nick even more stressed out than before.

"I'm happy to hear it." Max smiled, and seemed to truly mean what he said.

He'd always been devastatingly good-looking, even when they were in school. Now, as a man, confident and sure of himself, he was breathtaking. Not only was he tall, he was also lean and muscular. She hadn't exaggerated when she said he was in the prime of his life. His dark brown hair was short around the sides and back, but a little longer on the top. He wore a close-trimmed beard, but it couldn't hide his chiseled jaw or his well-formed mouth.

But it was his eyes that made him stand out among a group of men. Looking at them now made her insides get all warm and fluttery.

Piper forced herself to look away. She had no business getting butterflies over Max Evans anymore. She knew better, not only because he'd broken her heart, but because he had drawn a lot of attention as an NFL player. His good looks, coupled with his reputation with the ladies off the field, put him in the tabloids. He'd dated several beautiful women over the years, a couple models, a movie star, and more recently, Miss California, who was also the daughter of a successful California college football team's head coach, though Piper would never admit to knowing these details.

If given the chance, Max Evans would only break her heart all over again. When things got hard, he walked away. He had done it to her before and he would do it again. There was nothing that would ever persuade her to give him another chance.

He studied her, just like she was studying him, and she wished she was wearing something a little more appealing. She was only twenty-eight, but she felt as if she'd already lived a lifetime. Did it show? Could he see the fine lines around her eyes? The few gray hairs that had popped up in her long dark hair?

"Max?" A faint voice called to him from the front entry. "Are you here, son?"

"Mom." He let out a sigh and moved away from the bathroom door. "I have a few things I need to say to her."

Piper had to step aside to let him pass. He smelled of The One, by Dolce & Gabbana. She met his gaze as he passed and couldn't hide her surprise. The scent had been her favorite cologne in high school and she bought a bottle for him every Christmas as a gift. When she asked him if he liked it, he had told her it was okay, but he didn't wear it for himself. He wore it for her.

And he still wore it, even though she hadn't been around for ten years to smell it on him.

"Max?" Mrs. Evans called up the stairs, "Roberta says you're here."

"Coming," Max called back. He looked at Piper. "Can we talk later? We have a lot of things to discuss."

It was the last thing she wanted. "I don't think that's a good idea. We should leave the past where it belongs."

"I'm talking about the business, Piper. I have no idea what I've gotten myself into. I'm going to need a little guidance, if you're willing."

Heat warmed her cheeks as she nodded quickly. "Of

course." He was now her boss, after all. A prospect that felt a little too strange for her liking.

With one more rueful smile, he was gone.

Piper stood in the Garnet Room and realized she was breathing as if she'd just run up a flight of stairs.

Max Evans was back and she wasn't sure she was ready.

Chapter Two

The handrail was slick and smelled like lemon polish as Max descended the stairs. His mom stood in the entry with a huge grin on her face, while his eighteen-year-old brother, Tad, sat idly in an ornate chair, his phone in hand. He glanced up when Max appeared on the steps and lifted his chin in acknowledgment before returning his attention to his phone.

"Maxwell!" Mom opened her arms wide and waited for him to meet her at the bottom of the steps.

He smiled and lifted her off her feet in a tight embrace. "Hi, Mom."

She laughed as she returned his hug. "Put me down before you drop me."

Mrs. Anderson stood in the doorway leading into the dining room and Piper appeared at the top of the steps. Both watched the reunion silently, but neither made a move to join them.

Max set his mother on her feet and she lifted her eyebrows, giving him an excited look. She leaned in and whispered, "Were you surprised to see Piper?"

Surprised wasn't a strong enough word to describe how he felt standing in the same room as Piper. "Very."

"I hope you're pleased."

How could Max say otherwise with Piper close enough to hear? "Of course." What he wanted was to get his mother alone so he could really tell her what he thought about her meddling.

Mom looked him up and down, her brown eyes, so like his, taking a full measure as only she could. "You look too skinny."

"That's exactly what I thought," Mrs. Anderson said. "He needs more meat on his bones."

Mom patted his arm. "Now that you are home, we'll take care of you." Her face glowed like it hadn't in years—not since Dad died. She looked over at Tad. "Aren't you going to say hello to your brother?"

"I did," Tad said without lifting his gaze off his phone.

Mom rolled her eyes. "Put the phone away, Tad. It's not every day that you see your brother."

Tad sighed and turned off his phone. He unfolded himself from the chair and rose to clasp hands with Max. For the first time, they stood eye to eye and Max felt like he was looking at a younger version of himself.

"I'll be seeing him every day at practice from now on," Tad said, his voice and countenance as bored as before. "What's the big deal?"

Mom shook her head and matched Tad's sigh with one of her own. "Show a little enthusiasm, Tad. Your brother's come home and he's going to coach your team. How many of your teammates can say their brother is an NFL player?"

"*Ex*-NFL player," Tad corrected with emphasis. He

put his hands in his pockets and leaned against the banister. "With little to be proud of, if you ask me."

"Tad!" Mom's voice rose high with shock. "Max has a lot to be proud of."

Tad shrugged and glanced up the stairs, finally noticing Piper. A hint of a smile tilted his lips.

There was an edge to his brother that surprised Max. Tad used to admire him—it had almost been comical how much he looked up to him—but not anymore. Was it simply because Max had retired from the NFL—or was it something more?

"Don't mind him," Mom said with a wave of her hand. "He's a teenager." As if that explained away Tad's poor behavior. She motioned to Piper. "Come join us."

Piper acquiesced and stopped at the bottom of the steps. She offered Mom a tight smile. "Hello, Mrs. Evans."

Mom didn't seem to notice Piper's annoyance, but reached out and wrapped her arms around the younger woman. "How are you doing?" she asked. "Were you surprised when Max showed up?"

"Shocked," Piper said as she pulled back. "I wish you would have told me."

"Why?" Mom shared a giggly smile with Mrs. Anderson. "We knew you two would never agree to the arrangement if you'd known, but it seemed perfect. You needed a buyer and Max needed a place to live. It couldn't have been a better fit."

It was evident that both women adored Piper, and that the feeling was mutual, but Piper couldn't hide her frustration. She glanced at Max. "Just so you know, your mom and Mrs. Anderson are part of a group of ladies at Timber Falls Community Church with quite a reputation."

"A reputation?" Max frowned. What kind of a reputation could his mom have?

"As matchmakers," Piper supplied. "With Mrs. Caruthers as the ringleader."

"Oh, pish-posh." Mom laughed. "We're just helpful church ladies, that's all. It's our job to meet the needs of the parishioners. If we happen to bring two people together, all the better."

"I'm an innocent bystander," Mrs. Anderson claimed, putting her hands up in a gesture of surrender. "I just make the food."

Piper gave Mrs. Anderson a knowing smile. "You're not as innocent as you claim." A dimple appeared in Piper's right cheek. The sight of it made Max's breath pause. He was cast back to the first time he saw her at Vacation Bible School at the age of nine. He'd been sitting on a pew, waiting for the activities to start, when she walked into the sanctuary at Timber Falls Community Church. He'd never seen her before and he was immediately struck by her violet-blue eyes and the air of confidence she exuded, even at that young age. He hoped and prayed she would be assigned to his group, and when the volunteer pointed toward him, he sat up straighter. Piper walked over to the pew and sat down beside Max. She smiled and that's when he saw the dimple for the first time. It was so cute, and so endearing, he spent the next nine years of his life trying to make her smile—and he'd succeeded, over and over again, until the night he had betrayed her. Instead of smiling, that night she had cried.

"I just wanted to stop by and see how things are

going." Mom's smile was hopeful as she looked at Max. "And I wanted to chat with you for a couple minutes, if you have the time."

"Sure." He wanted to talk to her, too.

"Shall we go onto the porch?" Mom didn't wait for him to agree, but took his arm and directed him to a door under the stairs. "We'll be right back," she called over her shoulder to everyone in the entryway.

Mom wasn't a short woman, but next to him, she felt small. He had a natural instinct to protect her. After Dad had died, he'd been too preoccupied with his career to be there for her. Now, though, things would be different. It had been several months since he saw her last. She had brought Tad to the stadium in Minneapolis where Max had played his final professional game in January. His team had lost to Minnesota, but Max wasn't there to see the end of the game. During the second quarter, after being sent in to relieve the starting quarterback, Max had been sacked—and that was all he could remember. He'd suffered a concussion and been taken off the field. It took weeks to fully recover, and in that time, he'd made his decision to retire.

Max closed the door behind him and then followed his mom to one of the tall windows. This side of the wraparound porch was fully enclosed. Small wrought iron tables and chairs lined the long, wide room. The walls and ceiling were covered in beadboard which had been painted white, but the wide-plank floors were a dark gray, and the curtains at the windows were a soft yellow. The room smelled like fresh paint and window cleaner.

"You should have told me about Piper." Max wanted to tell her what he thought about her meddling before she could start in with what she had to say. She had a way of redirecting conversations to benefit her cause, which usually left him confused or forgetting what he needed to say. "You know things aren't good between us."

"That's precisely why I did what I did, but that's not what I want to talk to you about."

"I do." He crossed his arms and faced her. "The last thing I want to do is make Piper feel uncomfortable. In every sense of the word, this is her home. I might own the deed, but I can see that she and Nick poured their hearts into this place."

"Not Nick." Mom shook her head.

"What do you mean 'Not Nick'?"

"He didn't lift a finger here. Piper did everything."

Max frowned. "How is that possible? The place used to be a dump."

"They bought the house five years ago. Piper worked here every spare moment she had, while building a successful weddings and events planning business."

"Where was Nick?"

Mom fingered one of the gauzy curtains and didn't meet Max's gaze. She rarely got angry, but he could see something brimming in the depths of her eyes now. "Racking up more debt at the casino. He was gone almost every weekend."

"Seriously?" Max continued to frown. "How do you know?"

"Piper is like a daughter to me." She finally looked back at Max. "How could she not be? You two were close for most of your childhood and I was the only mother she really had. Even after you left, we stayed close." She put her hand on his forearm. "But don't repeat what I've said about Nick. Piper would be hurt and mortified. She's only told a few of her closest friends the truth."

"But wasn't he a construction worker? Why didn't he help her?"

"After long days of working on other people's projects, he didn't have any interest in helping Piper." She glanced toward the closed door where they'd just entered the room and then leaned closer to Max. "And, to be honest, I think Nick was resentful that Piper followed her dreams to buy this house. He never really wanted it."

A heaviness settled over Max, knowing how much Piper had endured the past few years. It couldn't have been easy, especially being married to someone who didn't share her dreams or goals.

"After Nick died, the community rallied," Mom said, a smile on her face. "The past four months, there have been hundreds of volunteers here to help Piper finish the house. Everyone hoped she could keep it and run it as a bed-and-breakfast, but there was no way she could wait for it to turn a profit. She had to sell."

"And that's when you called me."

Mom's eyes glowed with pride. "Thank you, Max. From all of us. Even though she doesn't own the house any longer, she was so happy to stay and manage it. I think she's hopeful that one day she can purchase the house again when she's in a better financial situation."

His mom had given him a lot to think about. There was a part of him that wanted to hand the deed back to Piper, but the truth was, he didn't have a thick bank account, either. He was comfortable, but he couldn't take such a big hit.

"Now." Mom set her face and squared her shoulders. "I have something I want to ask you."

Inwardly, he grimaced. He had a hard time saying no to his mom, which was why he now owned a bed-and-breakfast. "What is it?"

"It's about Tad." Sadness slanted her mouth at the corners. "I can't seem to reach him. He already has several scouts watching him and he's being recruited by half a dozen colleges."

Max knew as much. His brother had a better chance of going pro than Max had.

"I don't like what it's doing to him," she said. "It's going to his head, just—"

"Just like it went to my head." He didn't need her to say anything for him to know what she was thinking.

"You know I love you, Max, and that I'm so proud of you, but—"

"But I didn't make good choices."

She nodded.

"That's why I've come back," he told her. "To redeem those mistakes."

"You can't redeem your past by your own deeds." She studied him. "Only God can redeem you. You know that."

He had rededicated his life to God after his last concussion, and his mom had told him it was enough. But it didn't feel like enough. He needed to make it up to a lot of people.

"What would you like me to do?" Max asked.

"I want you to reach out to Tad. He respects and admires you—"

"He *used to* respect and admire me."

"He still does," she said gently. "He's just lost and

I can't find a way to get through to him." Her eyes pleaded with him. "Will you help?"

"I don't know if I can make a difference, but of course I'll try."

Relief flooded her face. "Thank you. Since your dad died, Tad has been craving a male role model." She wrapped her arms around Max's waist one more time and then said after a brief pause, "If you could find a way back into Piper's heart while you're at it, I'd love that, too."

He hugged her back and sighed. "It's not going to happen, Mom. I don't plan to get romantically involved with anyone, let alone Piper. There's too much between us." Ultimately, he'd only disappoint her again. Hadn't all his other relationships proved that to be true?

"I will never give up hope," she said.

"Ever the matchmaker."

"I do what I'm good at—and you will, too."

He wasn't sure what he could do for Tad or Piper, but he'd come back to make things right with the community and that's exactly what he would try to do.

Evening had fallen and Piper was weary in body and in spirit. All she wanted was a nice hot bath and her comfortable bed. Her feet ached from running up and down the steps all day, her back ached from making all the beds and her arms were sore from vacuuming thousands of square feet of rugs.

But it was her heart that hurt the most. Now that Max owned the bed-and-breakfast, it changed everything. Her one consolation when selling was the knowledge that she would stay and manage the business. It had been her lifelong dream. But now? Now, she would have to leave. She couldn't stay in the house with Max, no matter how much she wanted to operate the bed-and-breakfast. Too much had come between them.

Piper entered the kitchen and set a stack of dish towels in a drawer. The room smelled of sugar cookies, beef stew and fresh bread.

"I'm going to tuck in early." Mrs. Anderson covered a wide yawn with her hand, then untied her apron. "There's some beef stew warming on the stove and some bread toasting in the oven. I ate while you were upstairs vacuuming. I hope you don't mind."

"Of course not." Piper smiled, though her heart was heavy. She leaned against the center island. "You've done more than your share today. You should try to get some rest."

"I've only done my job." She patted Piper's hand. "You've done the majority of the work. You shouldn't push yourself so hard."

Piper placed her hand on her stomach and gave Mrs. Anderson a reassuring smile. "I'll be fine."

"Don't stay up too late." Mrs. Anderson yawned again and then crossed the wide room to her bedroom door. "And be sure to offer some of that supper to Max."

Before Piper could protest, Mrs. Anderson slipped inside her bedroom and closed the door.

Earlier, after his mom and brother left, Max had offered to help Piper get the house ready for the grand opening, but she had insisted she didn't need his help. It wasn't quite true, but she was still a little shaken from his sudden appearance and needed her own space to think about the ramifications. He was tired from the drive, so he went up to his third-floor apartment to get a few hours of sleep. The last thing she wanted was to go up there and offer him some supper. If she did, they'd have to talk and she wasn't ready to talk.

Piper turned off the stove and moved the stew to a trivet on the counter. The kitchen was part of a large private space with a living room and dining area that she shared with Mrs. Anderson. It connected to the formal public dining room with a swinging door that could be locked, if need be. At the back of the private living room was a door leading to the rear stairwell, giving them easy access to the second and third floors, as well as two other doors leading into Piper and Mrs. Anderson's spacious bedrooms.

Now that Piper had moved out of the third-floor apartment, this was her new home until the baby was born sometime around Christmas. Before that day, she had hoped to have enough money to rent a little place to call her own.

At least, that had been the plan. Now, with Max living just two floors above, she'd have to find a place sooner than she'd hoped. But there was no money. Every penny she'd made on the sale of the bed-and-breakfast had gone to pay off creditors. It would take several more months of hard work to pay off the rest.

There was a knock outside the dining room door. "May I come in?" Max asked.

Piper's pulse started to pound as she paused while taking a bowl out of the cupboard. "Of course," she croaked out. "Come in." She quickly glanced at her reflection in the chrome-covered toaster and tucked a stray piece of hair behind her ear. She had changed out of the paint-stained overalls she was wearing before, and put on a pair of black shorts and a simple white-striped shirt. She had also brushed her hair and put it up in a ponytail.

Max pushed open the door and stepped into the room. He had changed into a pair of close-fit jeans and a cotton hoodie. His hair was a bit mussed and his beard a little darker.

He was so good-looking it almost hurt. She forced herself to stop thinking about how handsome he was. It didn't matter what the man looked like. It mattered only how he behaved—and there were a few things Piper had read about Max in the gossip columns that had left her unimpressed. He was notorious for leaving a wake of broken hearts in his path.

His glance took in her and the living space in one broad sweep. "Does this house never end?"

A smile tilted one side of her mouth. She couldn't help it. "It's a lot bigger than I thought it would be when I was small." She motioned him to come in all the way.

"Is this where you and Mrs. Anderson live?"

Nodding, Piper went to the cupboard and pulled out another bowl. "Are you hungry?"

"Famished—and that smells amazing."

"You have one of the finest cooks in Timber Falls working for you." She filled both bowls and then put on oven mitts and took the bread out of the oven, all the while conscious of his presence.

"And fresh bread?" Max shook his head, coming farther into the kitchen. "I can get used to this."

Piper worked silently as she took out a couple of spoons and some napkins. How long did Max intend to stay? Was he back for good? Or was this only a stopping point on his quest for bigger and better things?

"Can I help?" he asked. "I feel like I've been useless all day."

"You can get out the milk and some cups."

The dishes were housed behind glass-front cabinets, so it was easy for him to locate the cups.

When all was ready, they brought everything to the small table tucked into the bay window and took a seat. Piper's hands trembled with the uncertainty of talking to Max again. She wasn't ready to discuss the past, nor was she ready to tackle the issues at hand. She'd had time to think—and she'd made some decisions—but it wouldn't be easy to share. At least, not yet.

Outside, dusk had just started to fall and there was a warm glow over the lush landscape just beyond the window, offering an intimate setting inside. A pretty white gazebo sat in the center of the yard and would one day be the site of small wedding ceremonies or bridal showers. All around them, lights were turning on in the other houses and the sounds of the neighborhood were beginning to quiet. It was a time for families to gather, to share the little nuances of their days together. Knowing the size of Timber Falls, it was safe to guess that Max would be discussed around most of those dinner tables. News of his arrival would have spread quickly.

"Would you like me to say grace?" Max asked.

Piper nodded and bowed her head.

"Lord, thank you for this day, for this food, and for good friends, both old and new. Amen."

"Amen," Piper whispered, suddenly not as hungry as she'd been before.

Steam lifted from their bowls as they dipped their spoons into the stew.

"Has Mrs. Anderson eaten?" Max asked.

"Yes. She's already gone to bed." It was early for the older woman, but Piper would not tell Max. He didn't need to know that she was probably trying to play matchmaker.

They ate for a few minutes before Max broke the silence. "My compliments to the cook."

"I'll be sure to tell her."

Max set his spoon in his bowl and then looked up at Piper. "I feel like I should apologize for buying your bed-and-breakfast."

"Don't be silly." She forced the stew down her throat. "You were a godsend." At least, that's what she had thought when she learned there was a buyer who was willing to pay top dollar and wanted her to stay on. If she had known it was Max, she might have questioned God's choice—just like she was doing now.

"I don't feel like a godsend." His eyes were so soft in the glow of the setting sun. "I feel like an intruder. I know how much this house means to you—has always meant to you."

There was a part of Piper that felt like she knew Max Evans inside and out. They'd grown up together, shared all their greatest hopes and dreams, their deepest hurts and fears. But ten years had passed, and both of them had changed a great deal. Neither one was the person they were at graduation. In almost every sense of the word, Max was a stranger to her.

She took another bite of stew before she spoke again. She needed to tell him what she'd decided and couldn't put it off any longer. "Every weekend is booked through the first of the year, so you shouldn't need to worry about income. I'll stay on for the next two weeks to get things up and running, and to give you time to find a new manager, but I think it'll be best for both of us if I leave."

Max lowered his spoon to the side of his bowl, his eyebrows coming together. "What? No. I don't want you to leave, Piper. This is your home, your dream. I didn't come to take it away from you."

"I know." She couldn't look him in the eyes, so she pushed a piece of beef around her bowl with the spoon. "I'm not mad. I just don't think it's a good—"

"I do. I only bought this place because my mom reassured me that I had a manager to take care of all the details."

"You can hire someone else."

"No one that will do as good a job as you." He leaned back in his chair. "If anyone should move out, it's me. If that's what has you worried, I'll—"

"It's your house now. I can't ask you to leave."

"It's not a big deal. I'll bunk with Tad for a few weeks until I find something to rent."

Piper finally looked at Max, a brow raised. "I'm not going to let you bunk with your eighteen-year-old brother. There's a very nice apartment, fully furnished, on the third floor that belongs to you. It would be silly to make you look for another place to rent."

"And there's a very nice apartment right here for you to live in." His gaze fell to the rise of her stomach for a brief moment. "I know you need the job and, more importantly, I know you want the job. Please don't quit, Piper."

Just the thought of leaving made her want to weep, but it was for the best—wasn't it?

"We're adults," he said. "Can't we find a way for this to work?"

Piper set down her spoon and clasped her hands on her lap, but didn't respond right away.

Max took a deep breath. "I've thought about what I would say to you when, or if, I ever had the chance."

"You don't need to say anything." She shook her head, not wanting to discuss the past—at least, not now, not when she was still reeling from his sudden appearance in her life.

"I made a lot of mistakes, Piper, and I have a lot of regrets, but when I look back at my life, the biggest regret I have is how I treated you."

She didn't want to hear what he had to say, but she couldn't walk away now. There was a part of her that didn't want to forgive him. He'd hurt her very deeply, especially knowing what he did about her past. His betrayal had wounded her to her core. A simple apology didn't feel like enough—yet, what more could he offer?

Nothing. A wound as deep as hers could not be healed by mere words. Nor could she open herself up to ever trust him again.

"I know there is nothing I can do to make things right between us," he said. "But I want to try. I know how much this house means to you and I want you to stay, for as long as you like. And, maybe someday, if you are able, I want to sell it back to you. I'll keep this house for as long as it will take."

Tears sprang to Piper's eyes, but she forced herself to hold them at bay. "You'd do that for me?"

Max reached across the empty space between them and gently put his hand over her clasped ones.

Piper held her breath as she met his gaze.

"I'd do anything in the world for you, Piper." He seemed to be trying to control his own emotions. "I know I hurt you, and more than anything, I wish I could go back and make different decisions, but it doesn't mean I stopped caring about you." He smiled and creases formed at the sides of his mouth. "You were my best friend—and to be honest, no one has ever replaced you. I've had a lot of acquaintances, and some friends through the years, but I've never met anyone who I could call my best friend." He paused, his smile dimming a bit. "I miss having a best friend. I miss you."

She could no longer hold the tears in check. One slipped down her cheek. She had missed him, too, for a long time, but she had learned to live without Max Evans in her life. The idea of trying to resurrect a relationship, after so much time and pain, was too much to even consider. She could never take that risk again, especially with a baby on the way. She needed to stay strong, both mentally and emotionally, so she could deal with the demands of motherhood. But, could they work together? He seemed genuine in his desire for her to remain—and, if it meant that one day she could own the house again, then that was a risk she was willing to take.

Piper wiped at her tears and unclasped her hands, forcing him to remove his. She sat up straighter, resolve strengthening her spine. "We are adults," she agreed. "And we should be able to work together." She held his gaze. "But that's all that we can ever be, Max. Coworkers. Nothing more. Ten years ago, our friendship died, and once something dies, it's lost to us forever."

The light in his eyes dimmed even more, but he nodded, as if accepting whatever she had to offer.

He was quiet for several minutes, but then he said, "I'm happy you'll stay, Piper."

Even though things weren't perfect, she was happy to stay, too.

Chapter Three

The next morning, Piper was out of bed and dressed for the day before seven. She hadn't slept well the night before, but there were so many tasks left to accomplish before the grand opening at three. She couldn't lie in bed, even if she had wanted to.

By one in the afternoon, she was utterly exhausted and was thankful when her friend Liv Butler appeared at the rear entrance of the house. "I've come with fresh flowers and brochures hot off the press."

Mrs. Anderson was busy making another batch of sugar cookies, claiming the three hundred she had made the day before wouldn't be enough. Max was on a ladder outside, cleaning an old bird's nest out of an eave of the house. Piper was seated at the little alcove desk under the back stairs, updating their Facebook page with some pictures to encourage people to stop by the open house between three and six before the first guests would check in.

"I'll be done in a second!" Piper called to her friend. She pressed Post and then shut the cover of her laptop.

Her back ached, so she stretched before she rose to greet her friend and business partner.

"These are for you." Liv handed over a large bouquet of flowers in an elegant vase. "Congratulations on the opening of the bed-and-breakfast."

Piper buried her face in the beautiful red roses and took a sniff. "Thank you."

"And," Liv said, holding up a brochure for their weddings and events business, "didn't these turn out amazing?" They had started their company right out of college, and though they were successful, it was more like a part-time job for the two of them. Timber Falls simply wasn't large enough to provide enough weddings and events for full-time work. Because of it, they didn't have an office building. Instead, they worked out of their homes, meeting with clients in their living rooms or at venues. She'd always dreamed of using the bed-and-breakfast as the headquarters of their business. What better place to meet with clients?

Piper took one of the brochures and quickly scanned the information. They had updated them with fresh photos and new information about the Warren House's availability for small weddings and events. "I love them. We can set them up in the visitors' information rack near the reception desk in the foyer."

"Great." Liv was tall and graceful and was always dressed well. No matter the occasion, she wore heels, and her blond hair was rarely out of place. She had once told Piper that she considered her appearance a billboard for her work as a weddings and events planner, as well as an interior designer—her other part-time work. Today was no exception. "I'll go put these in the rack and then I need to talk to you about our bridezilla."

Piper's shoulders fell. "Today? Can't it wait until after the grand opening is behind me?"

"I wish it could, but it's a time-sensitive matter."

Both ladies walked through the dining room and into the front foyer. Piper set the bouquet of flowers on the reception desk and Liv put the brochures in the only empty spot on the rack.

"What's so important we can't wait to discuss it?" Piper asked.

The front door opened and Max walked in.

Liv's eyes opened wide. "Max!"

Max grinned. "Hi, Liv."

"What are you doing here?" Liv had moved to Timber Falls her senior year and had graduated with them. She had been a friend, but she and Piper had grown closer when they went to the nearby community college. There, they'd both minored in business studies. Piper had majored in tourism and hospitality, while Liv had gone into interior design.

"I'm the new owner of the bed-and-breakfast," Max said as he hugged Liv. "Didn't Piper tell you?"

Liv shook her head, surprise still written all over her face. "I just got here." She looked at Piper. "Why didn't you say something? This is kind of a big deal."

"I thought you would have heard by now." Piper shrugged.

"If I had, I'm pretty sure I would have led with that information when I got here." She shook her head and looked between Piper and Max. "What a crazy turn of events."

Piper had no wish to continue this particular conversation, so she turned to Liv. "What did you need to tell me that couldn't wait?"

"Oh, it can wait, now that I know there's more interesting things to discuss." She eyed Max with curiosity, but Max seemed to sense Piper's unease.

"I'm just in here to take a quick shower and change my clothes," he said.

"You *live* here, too?" Liv's eyes couldn't get any wider.

"On the third floor." He pointed up the stairs as he walked toward them. "A reporter is coming by to interview me for the *Timber Falls Tribune* and then I'll be leaving later this afternoon for our first away game."

"You won't be here for the grand opening?" Liv asked.

Max shook his head. "I didn't know about it until I got here yesterday. If I had, I would have made other plans, but—"

"The team comes first," Liv supplied.

"Well, something like that." Max glanced at Piper. "Though, I'd prefer to stay and help. You could say I have a vested interest in the success or failure of the Warren House Bed & Breakfast now."

He didn't need to remind Piper. She was all-too aware of his hand in her dream.

"It was nice seeing you again, Liv." Max started up the stairs.

"You'll be seeing a lot more of me." Liv grinned.

Max took the stairs two at a time and was soon out of sight. The third-floor stairway door clicked shut and Liv grabbed Piper's arm. "What in the world, Piper? Max Evans is back in town and he's living in *your* apartment."

"Don't remind me—and it's his apartment now," she added.

Liv leaned eagerly against the registration desk. "How did it happen?"

Piper walked around the desk and took a seat on the stool. "I'd rather not talk about it, Liv. I didn't know he was the new owner until he showed up yesterday—and I'm still not sure how I feel about all of it. I'm choosing to focus on one day at a time."

Sighing, Liv glanced up the stairs. "He's even better looking now than in high school."

A twinge of jealousy turned in Piper's chest, but she chose to ignore it. She had no right to be jealous, or to be threatened by her pretty friend. For all she knew, Max was still dating Miss California.

"What did you need to tell me?" she asked Liv.

It took Liv a moment to focus, but then her lips thinned. "Carrie Custer left me a text and she's not happy with the venue she selected. She wants an outdoor wedding now."

"What?" Piper leaned forward on the stool, her mouth falling open. "An outdoor wedding in the middle of November?"

Liv shrugged. "If she wants it, her daddy will insist she have it."

"November, in Minnesota?" Piper had lived in Minnesota her entire life. Sometimes November could be beautiful and warm—other times, it could be frigid with a foot of snow on the ground. There was no way to predict the weather, and an outdoor wedding was a horrible risk to take.

"When your father is the mayor of Timber Falls," Liv said, "and also one of the wealthiest bankers in town, you get to have an outdoor wedding in November if you want."

Piper put her head down on her hands. In all the years they'd been planning weddings, they had never had such a difficult bride. Carrie Custer was not only young, just out of college, but she was also very spoiled. She'd been planning her wedding since last October and had completely changed her mind five times on theme, colors, locations, food, decor and the rest. "With only two and a half months to the wedding, she shouldn't be making such big changes."

"She said she has the right to change the location until the wedding invitations are sent out at the beginning of October." Liv rolled her eyes. "So, she wants us to come up with a list of suitable locations for an outdoor wedding by tonight."

"It's not possible." Piper lifted her hands in defeat. "I don't have the time—"

"Don't worry about that," Liv said. "I'll get her the list."

"But it's also the logistics of the thing. We'll have to plan for any and every possibility."

"If money isn't an option…" Liv let the words linger.

"I suppose you're right." Piper shrugged. "If she knows the risks she's taking, then who are we to say what she can and cannot have?"

"Alright." Liv crossed her arms on the high registration desk. "I'll come up with a list. If you think of somewhere, let me know, but if not, don't worry about it today. You already have enough on your plate with the open house. I just wanted to let you know."

The front doorbell rang and Piper straightened her back.

Liv took a step back and glanced toward the front door. "Looks like Larry from the *Tribune* is here.

Maybe you can get him to do an article on the open house, too."

"Larry is the sports writer," Piper said, coming around the desk to answer the door. "And besides, someone from the paper is coming by later during the actual open house to interview some of our guests and take pictures."

"It'll be interesting to see what makes the front page this week." Liv laughed, but Piper knew which news story would be more interesting to the local citizens of Timber Falls.

Max Evans was home. Nothing else could compare to that headline.

It was late, but several lights were on in the bed-and-breakfast as Max pulled his silver Lexus into the small parking lot on the north side of the massive house. The Lumberjacks had beat the reigning state champions, the Plainview Pioneers, in a close game and he was both exhausted and energized. He'd almost forgotten what it was like on a high school football field. It didn't match the size or magnitude of a professional stadium, but there was something extra special about an outdoor field under the brilliant lights, and a crowd full of mothers and fathers, grandparents, neighbors and friends cheering on their favorite player.

Max got out of his car and went around to pull out his duffel bag and clipboard. There were six other cars in the parking lot, probably belonging to their guests. Thankfully, the back stairs led all the way to the third floor so he wouldn't have to interact with strangers. That was Piper's job, and given her friendly, outgoing personality, she was the perfect person for the task.

His phone was on vibrate, but he could feel it ringing in his back pocket. After he set the duffel bag on the back steps, he pulled out his phone and glanced at the screen. Tom Sutton?

Max frowned. Why would his ex-girlfriend's father be calling him? He'd dated Margo Sutton for about six months before he'd decided to retire from the NFL. Her father, Tom Sutton, was the head coach of the Mid-State California Trailblazers. Max had been a big fan and had met Tom through some mutual friends. Tom, in turn, had introduced him to his daughter, Margo. At the time, Margo had been the reigning Miss California, but when her reign had ended, they had started to date—at least, until he'd decided to leave the NFL. Within a couple of days of Max's retirement, she'd broken their relationship with no explanations, but Max didn't need any. Without his status, she wasn't interested, and the truth was, he wasn't heartbroken. He'd been close to breaking it off with her, too.

But why would her dad be calling?

Tapping the green icon, Max brought the phone up to his ear. "Hello?"

"Max? Tom Sutton here. Have I caught you at a good time?"

Max was standing in the dark, outside the bed-and-breakfast. What better time to talk to the head coach of one of the most successful college football teams?

"This is a great time. What can I do for you?"

"I called to offer you a job."

The frank, no-nonsense statement made Max take a seat on the steps. "What kind of a job were you thinking?"

"I'm looking for a talent scout and you came to mind.

I remember several conversations with you regarding other players, both at college and professional levels. You have a good eye and I could use you on my staff. I'd like to give you a shot."

Max stared out at the dark yard beyond the small parking lot. A soft light glowed from the streetlamp at the intersection of Third Street and Second Avenue, and he could see the blue light of a television in a neighbor's home across the street.

"Max?" Mr. Sutton asked. "What do you think? How soon could you be here?"

Max could no longer sit, so he stood and began to pace, rubbing the back of his neck with his hand. "I just started a new coaching job today and I'm committed until the end of October, possibly November if the team goes to state."

"State? Are you coaching a high school team?" The incredulity in Mr. Sutton's voice grated on Max's nerves. "You're better than that, Evans."

Max stopped pacing and shook his head. There was no shame in coaching a high school team, especially when it was his hometown's. "My kid brother is a senior this year and the team needed a coach." He didn't add that he had blown the town's only opportunity for a state title ten years ago and he'd come back to redeem that mistake.

"That's a noble cause." There was a newfound measure of respect in Mr. Sutton's voice. "I had hoped to get you here sooner than that, but I can give you until Thanksgiving—for your hometown's sake. That is, if you want to come."

Max wasn't sure what he wanted. Seeing Piper again, being back in Timber Falls, where life used to be simple and where people actually cared about him, was really nice. But how long could he stay? Would he be content owning a bed-and-breakfast and coaching the football team three or four months out of the year? What would he do with the rest of his year? He had enough money to be comfortable, especially living in Timber Falls, but he wasn't opposed to making more.

"It's an honor to be asked," Max acknowledged. "But it's a big decision and I'd need some time."

Mr. Sutton was quiet for a moment. "If this has something to do with Margo, you don't need to worr—"

"No. It doesn't."

"Good, because I try to keep my personal life and my professional life separate and I ask that of my staff, as well."

"Of course."

"I need to find a scout, but I've got some time before the position needs to be filled. Let's talk again in a couple months. How's that?"

"Good. Thank you."

"Wonderful. We'll talk then." Mr. Sutton hung up the phone.

Max pulled his phone away from his ear and let out a deep breath. He hadn't expected a job offer from anyone after his retirement, least of all Tom Sutton. The job would be a good fit and it would be a way for Max to keep a pulse on the industry if he wanted to stay involved. But did he?

Picking up the duffel bag and clipboard, he walked up the short flight of stairs to the back door and into the rear entry. He wasn't sure how he felt about the offer. It was almost too good to be true—an opportunity anyone would be glad to take. But he had just wrapped his mind around being back in Timber Falls—and, truth be told, he was happy to be here. Happier than he'd been in a long time. And the prospect of reconciling with Piper, even if it just meant they could be friends again, was worth giving up a job in California.

But would it be necessary? Could he have both?

It was dark, so he flipped on a light and would have continued up to the apartment if the smell of marinara hadn't been wafting out of the kitchen. He hadn't taken time to eat supper and his stomach growled in protest.

"May I come in?" he asked with a light knock on the door.

"Come in," Piper called to him. "You don't need to knock every time you want to enter."

He pushed open the door and found Piper at the sink washing a large pot. "I feel like I'm invading your privacy if I just barge in here."

"This is a communal living space," she said as she rinsed the pot. "You're free to come and go as you'd like."

"Thank you." He set his clipboard on his duffel bag and left them by the door.

"How was the game?" she asked.

"It was tight, but we pulled out a win in the last quarter." He tugged at the hem of his long-sleeved shirt which sported the school's logo, two loggers' crosscut saws forming an X. "It felt good to be a Lumberjack again."

"Congratulations." She took a pan and set it in the soapy water. Next to her on the counter was a pile of platters, pitchers and various other dishes. Before tackling the pan, she stretched her back and winced.

"Shouldn't Mrs. Anderson be helping?" he asked.

"She got called away. Her granddaughter fell off a slide and broke her wrist, so Mrs. Anderson is at her son's house babysitting the other grandkids while her son and daughter-in-law are at the hospital."

"Ouch. I hope it's not too serious."

"Sounds like they'll have to place some pins." Piper used her shoulder to push some hair off her face. She looked pretty in a pair of black leggings, an airy cream-colored tank top and a pair of red shoes, which she'd kicked off to the side. "Hopefully she'll be home later tonight."

"Can I help you with those?" He couldn't just sit back and watch her work.

"I wouldn't mind some help." She nodded toward a dish towel lying on the counter. "If you could dry the dishes—"

"How about I wash and you dry, since you know where everything belongs."

Piper nodded and took her hands out of the soapy water. She dried them on the apron she wore. It was tied in such a way that it emphasized her baby bump. She had to be the cutest pregnant lady he'd ever seen. It suited her well. As an only child, with no mother since the age of nine, Piper had often talked about having a lot of children one day. She had always envied large, loving families, and told Max on several occasions that she would have her own someday.

When they'd been dating, he fully expected those children to also be his, and he'd wanted them as much as her. There was something profound about the idea of bringing a child into the world—one that was part of him and her. After she married Nick, he'd expected them to have a whole household of little ones by now. A part of him wanted to ask why she didn't, but he knew it wasn't any of his business.

"How are you feeling?" he asked, instead.

She glanced at him as she took the dish towel in hand. "My feet and back are a little sore, but I'll be fine."

"Pregnancy looks good on you." It was true. Not only did the roundedness of her stomach look adorable, but there was a glow about her that exuded life.

Her cheeks filled with color, but she didn't dip her head or show any signs of embarrassment at his compliment. If that was the case, he'd be sure to offer more.

"Thank you," she said.

"Do you know if you're having a boy or a girl, yet?"

"I'm choosing not to find out."

He nodded as he put his hands in the water, surprised at how hot it was. "I bet Nick was excited when he heard the news."

She lifted a platter out of the drying rack and didn't respond to his comment. Max glanced at her, thinking that she might not have heard—but the look on her face suggested she had.

"Didn't Nick want kids?" he asked softly.

Piper nibbled on her bottom lip as she dried the platter. "At first he did," she confided slowly. "We tried for kids right away, but after a couple years, I encouraged him to see a doctor."

Max continued to wash the dishes as he listened to her, not wanting to show any emotion, either way, in case it made her stop telling him the story.

"I had been to my doctor several times and had been reassured that I should have no trouble conceiving." She set the platter down and took up a glass pitcher. "Nick didn't want to admit the problem might be with him. We started to fight about the issue—a lot. Month after month, my dream of having a baby was dashed, but he refused to seek medical help."

A clock somewhere in the house chimed the hour as Max rinsed the pan he'd washed and set it on the drying rack.

"Everything snowballed from there. We had bought this place and were living on the third floor. I was pouring every spare moment, and dime, into the house and he pulled away a little bit more each day." She tucked a dark brown curl behind her ear and picked up the pan. "I was miserable. He was miserable. We fought all the time. When I finally talked him into seeing a doctor, five years had passed. That was about a year ago. It took several months to finally get pregnant." She stopped wiping the pan. "By then, he was indifferent to being a dad, our marriage was pretty much over and we were in serious financial trouble."

Her words were almost devoid of emotion. "I'm sorry, Piper."

She was quiet for a moment. "I always thought that somehow, we'd make it through. I knew things were bad, but I thought we'd have years and years to turn things around." She shook her head and swallowed hard. "If I would have known about the accident—known that we didn't have the luxury of time—I would have been less selfish and more understanding. I wouldn't have asked for so much."

"What did you ask for that was so selfish? A baby, a house and a happy marriage?"

"Those things sound like they'd be simple to attain, and most people have them, but I'm not entitled to any of them. They're gifts and I learned the hard way not to take any of them for granted." She set down the pan and took another dish. "I know it sounds a bit jaded, but the truth is, I've had to fight for everything I've ever wanted. Nothing has come easily to me, so I've learned how to square my shoulders and keep pushing forward. This house and baby were no different."

Max knew enough about her childhood to know that she'd been fighting since she was a little girl. Her mom had died of cancer when she was nine, but her parents hadn't told Piper her mom was sick until the week she died. They had kept it a secret for two years, thinking they were protecting her, but it had only caused Piper to mistrust the people closest to her. It was the reason she had made Max promise to always be honest with her, regardless of how much it hurt.

After her mom died, her dad had brought her to Timber Falls to start over and to take a new job. But he had started to drink and couldn't hold down a job for long. While other families attended activities and sports to cheer on their students, Piper had done everything alone. Max's parents had embraced her as a surrogate daughter, but it wasn't the same. The last thing she'd needed was for Max to hurt her, too.

But those things were in the past and there was no way for Max to change them. All he could do was focus on the here and now.

They worked in companionable silence for a few minutes and then Max asked, "How did the open house go? I'm sorry I couldn't be here."

"We ran out of cookies," she said with a slow smile. "Which made Mrs. Anderson both proud and embarrassed. She made over five hundred and all that we have left are the crumbs."

"Five hundred?" Max's eyes grew wide. "There were five hundred people here today?"

"More, probably." She shrugged. "Everyone was eager to see what this place looks like—and there were several who came hoping to get a glimpse of you."

Max paused his scrubbing. "Me?"

"Does that surprise you? You're the most famous person who's come out of Timber Falls since Esther Lund, the movie star."

"I'm very surprised. All this time, I thought the people of Timber Falls hated me for destroying their chance at a state championship title."

"You'll find that the people in Timber Falls are fiercely proud of and loyal to their own. They might be angry for a while, but their love always wins out." She glanced at him. "You might be pleasantly surprised to find that you're still a hero around here." She paused and her voice was a bit strained. "At least to most people."

From the tone of her voice, Max was certain she was one of those who no longer saw him as a hero, and rightly so. He just hoped he could change her mind, though he wondered if he had it in him to fix the damage he had caused.

Chapter Four

The sweet aroma of chocolate chip cookies wafted to Max's nose as he twisted the new bulb into the light socket above his head. Mrs. Anderson had just taken the last batch of cookies out of the oven and brought them into the front parlor where the guests could eat them at leisure. She'd also provided decaf coffee, hot tea and lemonade.

With a house full of guests, Max was happy to stay in the private quarters at the back and do the odd jobs on the list attached to the refrigerator. One of the lights had burned out in the kitchen and it was an easy enough task to complete. Plus, it gave him something to do on this first Saturday back in Timber Falls.

"Well," Mrs. Anderson said as she came back through the swinging door a couple minutes later. "I think my work for the evening is done. The guests won't require anything else until breakfast tomorrow morning."

Max folded the ladder he'd been using and laid it against the wall by the back door. He'd found it in the garage and would need to take it back out there before it got too dark.

As Mrs. Anderson set down the tray she'd been holding, Max glanced toward Piper's bedroom door. He had tried taking his time with the light bulb, hoping she'd make another appearance, but she'd slipped inside over an hour ago. Had she gone to bed for the night? It wasn't even seven o'clock yet.

"How about a game of Scrabble when I'm done here?" Mrs. Anderson asked Max.

It was the last thing he wanted to do with his Saturday evening. He opened his mouth to respond but was stopped when Piper's bedroom door opened and she stepped out.

She wore a cream-colored sweater dress with long sleeves, and a pair of tall brown boots. Her dark hair was long and flowing with loose curls. The outfit didn't hide her pregnancy, nor did it draw attention to it. She looked amazing—and clearly dressed to go out.

"Look at you," Mrs. Anderson said to Piper. "Don't you look amazing! Max, doesn't Piper look amazing?"

Max was speechless. She did look amazing, but he couldn't find the right words to say so. All he could do was nod.

"Thank you," Piper said as she closed her door and went to the side table where she grabbed her purse. "I'm already late, so I need to hurry."

"Where are you heading?" Max couldn't help but ask. It was none of his business, but his curiosity had the better of him.

"Our ten-year class reunion." She frowned. "Didn't you get the invitation?"

Max shook his head. "No."

"I'm sorry." She clutched her purse in her hands. "I just assumed you got the invitation and decided not to come. I would have mentioned it sooner if I had known." She studied him carefully. "You can still purchase a ticket at the door...if you want to come."

Did he want to go to their class reunion? He had lost touch with everyone over the years and didn't know how he'd be received. Would they give him the cold shoulder? Treat him like the villain he was? "I don't know if it's a good idea." He tried to laugh. "I'd probably be kicked out."

Piper lowered her purse. "You're the one who pulled away, Max—not them."

She was right. It was his own guilt and shame that had made him walk away from all his childhood friends. He'd used the excuse that they didn't want him to be a part of their lives anymore. But, if he was being honest with himself, it was his own fear of rejection that had kept him away—and threatened to keep him away still.

It was yet another example of his inability to stick around when things became difficult.

"Word has already spread that you're back in town." Piper motioned toward the door. "If you don't come, it'll be a blatant snub on your part."

She was always telling him the truth—regardless of how unpleasant it might be.

He'd come back to heal the past. Maybe his class reunion would be the place to start. "Can you wait about five minutes for me to change?"

Piper's eyes lit up at his words. "Sure. But hurry, I'm on the planning committee and am the master of ceremonies for the evening. I can't get there too late."

He didn't wait another moment, but raced up the two flights of stairs to the third floor and into his obscenely large apartment. It was far too big for one man and made him feel like a heel when he saw how small Piper and Mrs. Anderson's bedrooms were on the main floor. The third-floor apartment boasted four bedrooms, a large living room, dining room and kitchen, plus a couple alcoves inside the turret and gables. The slanted ceilings reduced the room sizes a bit, but it was still enormous for one single man.

Max hadn't completely unpacked his bags, so he had to rifle through one to find something decent to wear. If he was going to walk in with Piper, he needed to look presentable.

All his slacks were too wrinkled and he didn't have time to iron them, so he grabbed a pair of nice jeans, threw on a white button-down shirt, a gray vest to cover the wrinkles, and pulled on a black sport coat. He slipped his black shoes on while running his hands through his hair, and then he grabbed his wallet and cell phone as he ran out of the apartment again. He wasn't dressed as well as he'd like, but it was the best he could do.

When he slid to a stop on the bottom landing, where Piper stood waiting, he caught the look of appreciation on her face as she looked at him from head to toe. "You look nice," she said.

"Thanks."

"And you were fast, which is even better."

"I didn't want you to be late because of me." He opened the door to the outside and let her pass through. Not only did she look good, she smelled good, too. He took a deep breath and inhaled the scent.

She started toward the sidewalk, but he stopped by his car. "Do you want to ride with me?"

"The reunion is at the arts center downtown. It's only a few blocks." She nodded her head in the direction she was heading. "Want to walk with me?"

"I thought you were late."

"I'm late getting started. I don't have to be there until 7:30, but I wanted to give myself enough time to walk." She waited. "Are you coming?"

How many times had they walked together on these very same streets growing up? Max never thought he'd get the opportunity to do it again. "Of course."

They started toward the downtown, walking east along Third Street. Ahead of them, two blocks away, the historic courthouse stood large and imposing with the modern government center attached. Sunshine warmed the street, but it was no longer hot or unpleasant.

A wave of nostalgia overcame Max as he glanced at the familiar houses around him and caught sight of Piper beside him. Though she was small, she had been a tough little girl, often standing up for him as much as he did for her. Bullies, of all shapes and sizes, had crossed their paths over the years and they had done an equally good job of fighting them off together.

He couldn't help but smile as memory after memory came to his mind. His gaze hovered on her rounded stomach and he knew she would do just as well at being a mom. He wasn't surprised to find her tackling life as she always had, though his heart hurt knowing she must be weary of doing it alone.

"What?" she asked.

He shrugged. "Just thinking about the past."

A smiled tugged at her lips, revealing her dimple. "We had a good time, didn't we?"

Better than good. "It almost seems like a dream now."

Piper's gaze became wistful as she nodded.

They walked in silence for a couple more minutes and then Max asked, "Have you thought of names for the baby?"

"I haven't had much time to think about names." She smiled, though sadness lined the edges of her mouth. "If it's a girl, I've thought about naming her after my mom."

"Elaine?"

Her eyes brightened. "You remembered?"

"Of course I remember your mom's name." He nudged her playfully. "Piper, you were my best friend for most of my life. I remember a lot more than you think I do."

An awkward silence wedged between them and Piper looked away. "I'd call her Lainey for short," she said.

"And what if it's a boy?"

"I don't have a boy's name picked out."

"Maybe that means it's a girl."

She shrugged. "Maybe. Or maybe I don't want to think about raising a son without his father."

It was hard for Max to think about Nick being gone. He'd lost touch with him a long time ago, and had tried not to think about him being married to Piper—but it didn't dim his grief, especially knowing how much it hurt the woman at his side.

It didn't take them long to get to the arts center, which was housed in a historic brick building on the corner of Main Street and Second Avenue, near Ruby's Bistro. When they were kids, the building used to be a craft and hobby store, but when that had closed, it had been renovated for the arts association. Large plate glass windows allowed Max to see their reflection as they approached, and it put a smile on his face. He and Piper looked good together, and for a split second, he could almost see himself on a different path, if he and Piper had never broken up. If he had simply made one different choice, they could have been walking up to their class reunion, hand in hand, and the baby she was carrying could have been his.

But as quickly as the image flashed through his mind, he pushed it away. He had no right to play a game of what-if in his mind. He had made his choices and had been living with them for ten years. And, besides, he was in no position to be a dad or husband. He didn't even know where he'd be in four months when Piper's baby was born.

"Ready?" she asked as they stopped outside the door.

"As ready as I'll ever be."

She smiled and shook her head, allowing him to open the door for her.

Megan Galloway, the class secretary, sat at the registration table near the front door. Her eyes opened wide at the sight of Max and she stood. "Max!" With a squeal of delight, she rounded the table and grabbed him in a hug, bouncing up and down the entire time. "You came! You came!"

Max looked at Piper over Megan's shoulder and found her hiding a grin.

If Megan's reaction to having him join their reunion was any indication, he had nothing to fear.

* * *

Piper stood back as the eight reunion committee members came from all parts of the building to say hi to Max. Most of them were classmates who had returned to Timber Falls after college to settle down and raise their families.

"Why didn't you tell us Max was coming?" Amber Eckert asked Piper as she came to Piper's side. "I didn't see his name on the registration list."

"I'm just as surprised as you are." Piper shrugged. Even though it had been forty-eight hours since he'd shown up at the bed-and-breakfast, she was still a little off-kilter with the whole thing.

"Either way, it's pretty amazing." Amber sighed. "I can't wait until everyone else shows up. They'll all be so surprised."

Max stood amid the group of their old classmates and smiled politely, but Piper knew him well enough to see that he wasn't enjoying all the attention. That was one thing she'd always liked about Max. Even in high school, when he'd been the star quarterback and all the college scouts had come to watch his games, he had never once acted better than anyone else—at least, not until the end of the football season when there was talk of him being good enough to go professional. But before that, he had been voted homecoming king and most likely to succeed. He had been everyone's friend and no one's enemy. That was why his betrayal had been so hard on everyone. No one saw it coming— least of all, Piper.

"Come on, people!" Samantha Rainy called out to the group, her no-nonsense demeanor the same as it had always been. "We have a reunion to run. Everyone to their posts. You can visit with Max later."

As each person reluctantly left his side, Max's gaze found Piper's again. "What can I do to help you?" he asked her.

"Don't forget your registration!" Megan called to Max in a singsong voice, waving him over to the registration table. "I can help you with that here."

Max went to the small table where Megan sat and dutifully paid for his ticket.

"And here's a name tag." Megan giggled. "But I don't think you'll need to wear it. Everyone remembers Max Evans."

Max smiled uncomfortably and stuck the name tag to his coat. "Just in case," he said.

"Here's your name tag." Megan handed one to Piper. "Put it somewhere prominent so people don't have to guess who you are."

"How could anyone not know who Piper is?" Max asked with a grin.

Piper smiled to herself and took the name tag.

"Do you need help with anything?" Max asked Piper again.

"I'm the master of ceremonies, so my job won't start until later." She led him from the reception area into the main gallery where the reunion would be held. "I did a lot of the planning leading up to the event."

Instead of paintings on the brick walls, the decorating committee had blown up pictures from their yearbook and placed them around the room. The black-and-white images cast Piper back ten years and made her pause.

"Wow," Max breathed beside her. "I haven't seen these pictures since we graduated."

The committee members were in various places throughout the room, putting centerpieces on the tables, arranging the prizes for the drawings and attaching purple and black balloon bouquets on the stage. People were pretending not to watch Max as he and Piper walked over to the pictures, but he was clearly distracting several of them.

A hundred memories flooded Piper's heart as they took a stroll down memory lane.

The pictures were taken at all sorts of events their senior year. Some were taken at games, others in the commons at lunchtime, a few in the parking lot preparing for the homecoming parade, several in different classrooms with favorite teachers, a couple in the auditorium for the spring musical and dozens of other places. Nick was in a few of them, his grinning face a harsh reminder to Piper of what she had lost.

"Look," Max said, his voice a bit quieter than usual. He pointed at the biggest picture, which was in the middle of all of them. "It's us."

Piper stopped and stared. It was a picture of Max and Piper standing on the football field during homecoming, with Nick and the other homecoming court in the background. Max and Piper had been voted king and queen and Max was wearing his Timber Falls Lumberjacks football uniform, his crown sitting lopsided on his head. Piper was wearing a formal gown with a crown on her head and a cape over her shoulders. But they weren't looking at the camera; instead, they were grinning at each other.

"It feels like a lifetime ago," Max said, almost to himself.

It did feel like a long time had passed, but Piper could remember what she'd been thinking at that very moment. Though she was only seventeen, she knew exactly what she wanted out of life and who she wanted to grow old with. She had never trusted anyone more than she did Max, and not once had he broken that trust. She was deliriously happy the night she was crowned homecoming queen and had felt like she was floating on air.

But then she remembered what happened when she got home that night. She had found her dad passed out on the recliner again with an open bottle of gin at his side, and even though he hadn't come to any of her other school activities since seventh grade, she'd been bitterly disappointed that he'd missed her senior homecoming.

Her life might have looked good on the outside, and almost ideal in this picture, but she'd still had a lot of problems at home with her dad. He had not held down a steady job since her mom had died, and Piper had taken a job at the local grocery store on nights and weekends just to pay their rent and put food on the table.

"These pictures don't tell the whole story, do they?" Piper asked, hearing the bitterness in her voice, though she didn't intend to dredge up the harder memories from her past. "With each good memory, it seems there are a couple bad ones mixed in."

"Piper." Max's voice was full of regret. "I'm sorry—"

Piper shook her head. "I was thinking about my dad mostly." Though she couldn't stop herself from thinking about how much Max had hurt her a couple months after this picture was taken, or how Nick had come to her soon after and confessed how he'd always felt about her. She'd been in so much pain, she'd turned to him, but knew their relationship had always been a little lopsided because her heart had belonged to Max for the first few years. She didn't want to admit the truth, but she knew part of Nick's unhappiness was the fear that she had never stopped loving Max.

She put her hand on her rounded stomach and chose not to talk about any of those memories. There was no point in bringing them up again. Instead, she chose to talk about the present. "Even now there are good things mixed in with the bad. This pregnancy is one of them. I'm excited to be a mom after years of disappointments, but I never thought I'd be a single parent. Or think about the bed-and-breakfast. I'm thrilled it's finally open and it's even better than what I dreamed— but it's not mine. Pictures rarely capture the heart and soul of a person, do they?"

Max studied the picture of them together, a dozen different emotions playing across his handsome face. "No, they don't—but in this moment, at homecoming, I didn't think my life could get any better. This picture perfectly captured my heart and soul when it was taken."

"Moments are fleeting," she said wistfully, thinking that by the age of twenty-eight, she had already lost her mom, her dad and her husband. "I suppose this picture should remind us to not take anything for granted and to be thankful for each blessing, no matter what might come our way later on."

Max turned his gaze to Piper and he smiled. "I've always loved your optimism. You find a silver lining in almost everything."

It hadn't always been easy, but Piper had learned at

a young age that if she couldn't find something positive in each situation, she'd drown in a pool of self-pity. Even now, she could focus on being a single mom, or on the loss of her bed-and-breakfast, but neither of those things would change if she was upset. She needed to save her energy for what really mattered, and at the top of her list was erasing the debt so she could find a place to live when the baby was born.

But she didn't want to think about any of that tonight. Tonight was for good memories.

"Max Evans!" A former football teammate entered the main gallery and his voice echoed off the wood floor and tin ceiling. He was a big guy who had grown only bigger since high school. He rushed across the room and grabbed Max in a bear hug, lifting him off the floor. "What are you doing back in Timber Falls, buddy?"

Max laughed as he was put back on the ground, and soon he was surrounded by old teammates again, all of them clamoring to hear from their classmate-turned-NFL player. Piper thought how strange it seemed that Nick wasn't there, in the midst of his old friends. If it had been high school, Nick would have been right beside Max the whole time.

Soon Liv arrived and their old group of girlfriends gathered around a table to talk and share memories—though they weren't nearly as loud as the football players.

Piper tried to ignore Max and his buddies, but no matter how much she tried, everyone kept bringing up his name and all the antics she and Max had gotten into when they were kids.

"I don't think I have a single memory of Max that

doesn't involve Piper," said Roxanne Caruthers Downs, one of their longtime church friends. "No matter where Piper went, there was Max, and vice versa."

The table of ladies laughed and Piper wondered if Max's name would have come up less if he wasn't there. A few people brought up Nick's name, and how much they wished he could have been at the reunion, but the majority of their classmates seemed uncomfortable talking about his death. He was the first of their class to pass away and Piper knew it was a hard reality for a lot of people to deal with—her included. The reason they had postponed the reunion to Labor Day weekend was because their original date was just a few weeks after Nick's unexpected death.

Soon it was time for Piper to go onto the stage and start the program. She had never been shy about public speaking before and wasn't now, but being onstage gave her a good look at the room and she found that most of their class was congregated in the corner where she'd left Max a half hour ago.

"Can I have everyone's attention, please?" she said into the microphone. "If you could please find a seat, the caterers are ready to serve the meal."

It took a few minutes, but most people complied and found a place to sit—everyone, but a couple diehard Max Evans fans who ignored her and kept talking to him.

"Max isn't going anywhere, Brady," Piper said into the microphone. "And your wife is calling for you to come and sit down."

Brady's wife was waving at him from the front of the room, and when she was pointed out, her cheeks turned a crimson red. Everyone started to laugh and Brady hightailed it to his wife's side.

"Sorry!" Max called out to Piper as he looked for a place to sit while the room quieted.

As Piper shared some of the housekeeping details of the evening, several people motioned for Max to join them, but he moved to the table where Piper had been sitting with Liv and sat there, instead. He put his forearm on the back of the seat Piper had been occupying, and when Megan came up and tried to take the seat, Max shook his head and indicated Piper—apparently letting Megan know the seat was taken.

Piper hadn't even realized that Max knew where she'd been sitting earlier. He'd been so preoccupied with his friends, she just assumed he'd stay with them. But he wanted to sit with her.

Despite all her misgivings and uncertainties, her heart did a little flip-flop, and she felt like she was back in the school cafeteria again, being chosen and noticed by a guy who made her pulse skitter.

It was a good feeling—but she had to remind herself that she wasn't in school anymore, and she had a lot more at stake.

No matter how much Max still made her pulse gallop, she had to protect her heart, for her sake as well as her child's. More now than ever, she needed to know who she could trust and who she couldn't—and Max was already in the untrustworthy column.

She couldn't risk him walking away again when it mattered the most.

Chapter Five

"What do you say, Max?" Tom Treadway asked as the last of their classmates stood outside the arts center as the door was being locked by a staff member. "Would you like to go with a bunch of us over to Ed's Sports Bar for a couple of drinks?"

Max's ears were ringing with all the laughter and conversation that had buzzed around his head the past three hours. Piper stood to the side with the reunion committee, going over a couple of details, but she glanced in Max's direction after Tom's invitation.

It was late and dark, and he had no desire to join the others or leave Piper to walk home alone.

"Thanks for the invitation," Max said to Tom, reaching out to shake his hand. "But I think I'll head home. Let me know the next time you're in town and we'll get together."

Tom nodded, though it was clear he was disappointed. "Okay, buddy. Another time. It was great to see you."

"You, too."

The group walked down the street, toward the sports bar, laughing as they went.

"Thanks for all your hard work," Piper said to the committee members as they all broke apart. "I'll see you next week for our wrap-up meeting."

"Bye, Max!" Megan waved. "We'll see you again soon."

"Bye." Max waved at everyone as they walked toward their cars. "Thanks for the great reunion."

"It was my pleasure," Megan said with a wink.

Piper laughed and shook her head as she joined Max and they started to walk back to the bed-and-breakfast. "Some people never change."

"In some situations," he said, playfully tugging on her long hair, "it's a good thing." He'd loved watching Piper with all their old friends. It felt like a time machine had taken them back to high school for a few brief hours.

"Are you saying *I* haven't changed?" she asked.

"In all the ways that matter, you're exactly the same as you've always been."

"I feel like I'm a completely different person." The soft glow of the streetlamps illuminated her beautiful violet-colored eyes as she sighed.

"You're still confident, smart, kind, selfless, funny—"

"Okay, okay," she laughed, clearly uncomfortable as she laid her hand on his arm to stop him from listing her attributes. "You have no need to lay on the charm with me, Max Evans."

He smiled and loved seeing her smile, too. "It was fun being back with everyone and remembering all the good times we had together."

"It was a good night."

"I'm amazed that with everything else you had going on, you still managed to be on the reunion planning committee." He shook his head. "Anyone there would have understood if you needed to step down."

They came to a crosswalk and waited until the red light changed and then crossed the street. There weren't a lot of cars on a Saturday night in downtown Timber Falls. A couple of the bars and restaurants were open, and the movie theater was still running its late shows, but all the other businesses were closed.

"I needed something to occupy my mind right after Nick died, so I refused to give up any of the activities I was involved in," she said quietly. "Even though Nick wasn't home much before he died, and I was used to being alone, after his death, I was completely on my own for the first time in my life. I didn't like how that felt—I still don't—so I stayed as busy as possible."

"From what my mom told me, it sounds like the community rallied by your side."

"They did." She nodded, appreciation shining from her face. "Church friends, neighbors, classmates, even people I didn't know showed up to help at the bed-and-breakfast. People brought meals and donated furniture, and Liv started an online fundraiser where people could give money. Even though I felt all alone in the world, the community showed me that I wasn't alone—not really. It helped more than they'll ever know."

Guilt washed over Max again. "I wish I had known." How had he missed something as devastating as his friend's death? Had he been too preoccupied with his own life to pay attention to others?

"I know you do," she said, her voice gentle. "But please don't feel bad. You came right when you were needed most, to buy the bed-and-breakfast." She took a couple of steps. "Besides, we all have regrets and it doesn't help to keep beating ourselves up over the mistakes we made." She paused and looked ahead at the dark street. "As long as we learn our lessons, that's what really counts."

Had he learned his lessons? He carried around a lot of regrets, but was that the same as learning from his mistakes?

They continued to walk down the dark side street, past a parking lot behind the buildings on Main Street, but a group of kids standing near the back of the theater caught Max's attention. A nearby streetlamp gave him just enough light to recognize at least one of the students—and what he was doing.

"Hold on a second," Max said to Piper, his voice grave. He put his hand out to stop her. "I think that's Tad and a couple of his friends."

It was clear, even from where Max was standing, that they were smoking a vape pen. The plume of vapor rose in a large cloud over their heads.

He moved toward his brother and Piper followed.

The group of kids noticed Max and Piper almost immediately and started to whisper chaotically while Tad shoved the vape pen in his coat pocket.

Deep disappointment sliced through Max. He was well aware of the penalty for using, or being in the possession of, a controlled substance. It was the reason Max couldn't play in their championship game—though he had been using alcohol and not nicotine. The first offense disqualified a student from two interscholastic contests, or two weeks, whichever came first.

Tad had a lot going for him, especially on the football field. Why would he take any chances on throwing that away?

Thankfully, Tad was the only one in the group on the football team. If there had been others, their team would be in a lot of trouble for the next two weeks.

"Hey, Max." Tad gave Max an uncomfortable and awkward greeting. "You know my friends from grade school, but have you met my girlfriend, Shelby?"

Max recognized Tad's friends, though they were all much older than the last time he'd seen them. The blond-haired girl standing next to Tad smiled and gave Max a nervous wave. "Hi."

Max hated being the bad guy, but there was no other way. "Tad, I saw the vape pen. I'm going to need you to hand it over and then I want everyone to go home." He looked at all the kids, disappointment weighing down his voice. "You guys better prepare your parents, since all of you will be hearing from the principal on Monday."

"Aw, come on, Max!" Tad shook his head, his face turning into a scowl as he handed over the vape pen. "We weren't doing anything you wouldn't have done in high school. Lighten up."

"I never smoked in high school, Tad." Or any other time in his life. "It's not a good choice for many reasons, least of all is because it'll disqualify you to play in this week's and next week's games."

"Give me a break!" Tad scoffed and looked at his friends, pointing his thumb at Max. "This coming from the guy who got disqualified for drinking the night before the championship game."

Tad's friends didn't laugh with him and Piper shifted uncomfortably.

His little brother's comment hit its mark and made Max feel like a complete loser. But he couldn't let his mistakes keep him from pointing out his brother's. "And that's exactly why I can stand here right now and tell you smoking, or any other controlled substance use, is a bad idea." His mom wanted him to be a good example for his brother. The only way he could do that was to show Tad what not to do. "Nothing good can come from it, and if you're not careful, you could face the same regrets that I do."

Piper was silent next to Max, another reminder that it wasn't just the championship game he had lost because of his foolishness.

"I want everyone to go home," Max said, his pulse escalating. "And that includes you, Tad. I'll call Mom to let her know you're on your way."

"You're a jerk," Tad said, pushing past Max with his shoulder. "Why don't you go back to where you came from?" He paused and laughed sardonically again. "Oh, that's right, you can't. You're not only a fraud, but you're a quitter, too. The NFL won't take you back." Tad took his girlfriend's hand and pulled her along with him toward his car.

Anger pulsed in Max's veins. "Tad!"

His brother didn't stop or respond, but got into his car and slammed the door. His girlfriend looked uncertain for a second before getting into the passenger side.

The second the door closed, the old familiar feeling to walk away from the mess started to creep into Max's chest. He had done it a dozen times in the past ten years in romantic relationships, his career and even with his family—especially with his family. He'd always had a good excuse to leave and hope the problem didn't follow him.

For the most part, it worked—but what kind of a cad would he be if he didn't fight for his brother? Max couldn't keep ignoring the problems around him, no matter how much he wanted to pretend they didn't exist. Eventually, he'd have to face them and they'd be worse than ever.

"I'm sorry, Max." Piper let out a sigh. "He doesn't know what he's talking about."

Max shook his head, his shoulders drooping as he watched his brother's car pull out of the parking lot. "He knows exactly what he's talking about—and he knows exactly where to aim his ammunition."

Piper reached through the darkness and clasped her hand around his.

It wasn't a romantic gesture, but a comforting one. She'd done it hundreds of times in their youth. Offering reassurance was as natural to Piper as breathing.

"Don't let his anger steal your confidence," she said quietly, but with conviction. "He was in the wrong here, not you. You've already been punished for your transgressions. He was just trying to deflect his own mistakes to derail you from following through with his consequences."

Max's disappointment and frustration began to fade in the light of Piper's words.

"Come on," she said, tugging him toward the sidewalk. "It's late and my feet hurt."

He followed her, and when she let go of his hand, he had to fight the urge to reach out and take it again. He had missed Piper for so many reasons, but her calming presence was one of the things he missed the most. There had been countless times in the past ten years he wished she was by his side to offer some wisdom or insight, or to just be a voice of reason in difficult situations.

He had a feeling his life would look a lot more promising if she had been with him.

The week passed quickly and Piper was thankful the bed-and-breakfast was empty. By Thursday, there were so many things she and Mrs. Anderson needed to prepare before the onslaught of guests arrived for the big arts and crafts fair. It was the largest annual event held in Timber Falls, with over a hundred thousand visitors descending upon the small town for the weekend. Six hundred vendors set up booths along the streets and in the parking lots, and there were dozens and dozens of great food booths. It had always been Piper's favorite weekend of the year, but this year was a little different now that she was managing the bed-and-breakfast.

"The drier just buzzed," Mrs. Anderson said as she came into the Diamond Room where Piper was just finishing cleaning the bathroom. "I need to vacuum the rugs downstairs, but I can help you make beds before I need to run to the grocery store."

"The beds can wait," Piper said. "I still need to finish two more bathrooms and vacuum all the carpet upstairs."

Piper had been busy earlier in the week with her weddings and events business and had put off the cleaning until the last minute. Mrs. Anderson would have done most of it, if her son and daughter-in-law didn't need help with emergency childcare that week. Max had been home a couple evenings, but Piper didn't want to ask him for help. Not only was he busy with his coaching, but he had hired Piper and Mrs. Anderson to do all the work. It wouldn't be right to ask him to do what he was paying them to do.

"Do you mind if I run to the store now?" Mrs. Anderson asked. "I'd like to go before five when it becomes busy with weekend shoppers."

"Go ahead." Piper pushed aside a tendril of hair that had fallen over her forehead. "The beds aren't going anywhere."

Mrs. Anderson grinned, but Piper could see the fatigue around her eyes. "I'll be as quick as I can."

Piper nodded and picked up her cleaning supplies to go to the next bathroom. Her phone buzzed in her back pocket, so she set down the bucket and pulled her phone out. It was Max.

"Hello," she said. Max had never called her phone before and her pulse picked up a steady tempo now. Was something wrong?

"Hi, Piper." He sounded a little breathless, like he was walking. "I'm in a bind and I was wondering if you and Mrs. Anderson could help me out."

"Sure." Piper stood and stretched her lower back. "What can we do?"

"We have our first home game tomorrow night and after what happened with Tad, the team could really use a morale boost. I know this is last-minute, but I was wondering if you and Mrs. Anderson could whip up a quick batch of spaghetti for the team. It doesn't have to be fancy. They can eat off paper plates."

Piper stared at the unmade bed in the beautiful Diamond Room, her back suddenly hurting more than before. "Whip up a quick batch of spaghetti?"

"Yeah. There are about ten coaches and forty players—minus my brother who's been suspended from the team for two weeks." His voice was heavy and Piper knew how much it hurt him to have Tad miss their first home game of the year. "Some of the players have a pretty big appetite, so I'd double the batch, just to make sure. If Mrs. Anderson could make some cookies, too, that would be great. You'd really be helping me out."

Piper sank into a chair near the fireplace in the bedroom. She hadn't mentioned the important weekend coming up to Max, and she doubted he even remembered the big craft fair. No doubt he had no idea how busy she and Mrs. Anderson were.

"I know I'm asking a lot," Max said to Piper. "And I'd owe you big-time. I already extended the invitation to the team. They're showering and will be there in about an hour." He hesitated. "If that's not enough time for you, I can keep them busy tossing a few footballs around in the yard while I come in and help get supper on the table. Or, I can just order some pizzas and pick them up on the way."

It was Max's house and she and Mrs. Anderson were his employees. He wasn't out of line asking her for a favor.

"That many pizzas would be too expensive." She stood, needing to catch up to Mrs. Anderson before she left for the grocery store. "I'll run up and grab everything we need for spaghetti. I can't promise it'll be ready in an hour, but we'll do our best."

"Thanks, Piper. I'll reimburse you for all the costs, so don't worry about that. I appreciate it more than you'll ever know."

Piper pressed the red button and took a deep breath, overwhelmed with all the work she needed to do. She could have told Max to just order pizzas, but what was better than a home-cooked spaghetti dinner the night before a game? Max's mom used to host them all the time when Max was in high school. It was one of Max and Nick's favorite nights of the week, gathering together with all their friends. No doubt Max wanted to create the same atmosphere for his team. Besides, if Mrs. Anderson knew that she had told Max to order take-out pizzas, she'd probably hyperventilate. If food was a love language, it would be at the top of Mrs. Anderson's list.

There was no time to lose. Piper rushed down the hallway and then used the back stairs to enter the private living area. "Mrs. Anderson!" she called as she rushed in.

Mrs. Anderson stepped out of her bedroom, concern in her eyes. "What's the matter?"

Piper quickly explained Max's phone call, and just like Piper guessed, Mrs. Anderson was on board to make the meal.

"It's not ideal timing," she conceded, looking around the kitchen with a calculating gaze. "But I think we can do it. I have everything I need to make cookies, we just need the ingredients for spaghetti."

"I'll run to the store and purchase what we need."

Piper grabbed her purse off a side table. "We'll need to feed over fifty people."

"Oh, dear," Mrs. Anderson said. "That's a lot—but I've fed more." She pulled an apron from the hook near the pantry door. "I'm always up for a challenge."

They had so many things on their to-do list, they'd be up into the wee hours of the night, but Piper shoved it all to the back of her mind and dashed out the door.

In a half hour, she was back at the bed-and-breakfast with four gallons of milk, ten pounds of ground beef, a hundred ounces of spaghetti noodles and a dozen jars of premade sauce. Mrs. Anderson would balk at the idea of using store-bought marinara, but there wasn't enough time to make it from scratch.

"I just put the second batch of cookies in the oven," Mrs. Anderson said, perspiration on her brow. "And the big stockpot is full of water, heating on the stove."

Piper's stress level was as high as it had been in a long time. Her pulse thumped in her wrists and she was breathless as she set the first few bags of groceries on the counter. "I felt like I was on the *Supermarket Sweep* show. I've never run through the grocery store like that before. There was more than one curious shopper watching me."

"All's well that ends well," Mrs. Anderson said, hardly paying attention to Piper as she started to unload the grocery bags.

"Then let's make sure this ends well." Piper smiled. "I'll go get the rest of the groceries."

Right on time, half an hour later, the cars started to pull up to the street in front of the bed-and-breakfast. The high schoolers got out of their vehicles, and without being invited, started to toss several footballs around in the large side yard.

The back door opened and Max stepped into the room. "I hope I didn't ask too much," he said when he saw them scurrying about in the kitchen.

Piper hadn't had enough time to freshen up her appearance before Max came home. Her hair was a mess, she was wearing her paint-stained overalls, and her face and back were moist with perspiration. But, at the moment, the only thing she cared about was getting the football team fed.

"Wow." Max came into the kitchen and stared at the mound of cookies on a platter, the stockpot full of cooked pasta and the marinara bubbling on the stove. "I had no idea you'd be ready by the time I got here."

He smiled at them, but when he noticed their harried expressions, his smile faded.

"It wasn't easy," Mrs. Anderson said, wiping her hands on a dishcloth. "But we got it done."

"If there's anything I can do to help," Max said, "please let me know."

Piper tucked a stray piece of hair into her messy bun. "I think we've got it all covered. As soon as everyone is here, we can start to feed them."

"You two deserve the rest of the night off." Max set down his duffel bag. "I'll have the team clean up the kitchen for you."

"I wish we could take off the rest of the night," Mrs. Anderson said. "But the house is fully occupied this weekend and several people asked for early check-in tomorrow morning."

"Tomorrow morning?" Max looked from Piper back to Mrs. Anderson.

"The arts and crafts fair is this weekend," Piper reminded him. "It'll be the busiest weekend of our year."

Max closed his eyes and tilted his head back. "I completely forgot. I'm sorry, ladies."

Piper began to knead her lower back, which ached from being on her feet all day. She grinned at Mrs. Anderson. "All's well that ends well, right Mrs. Anderson?"

"After the guys eat," Max said, "I'm putting them to work for you. They can vacuum the rugs, make the beds, fold the towels—you name it, they'll do it."

Piper shook her head. "That's not necessary—"

"I insist." Max rolled up his sleeves. "You two need to put your feet up. I'll make sure the guys get fed and then when you're rested a little, you can give us orders."

Piper wouldn't hear it. "Max, it's really not—"

Max took her by the hand and drew her out of the kitchen. When she was in front of him, he put his hands on her shoulders and directed her to the sofa. "I won't take no for an answer. I'll make you a plate of food and you can sit here and enjoy it while the rest of the team eats."

Piper sat on the sofa and watched as Max brought Mrs. Anderson into the sitting area.

"I'm serious," he said. "You two do more than your fair share. We've got this."

Mrs. Anderson sat on the wingback chair next to the sofa and sighed. "I could use a little breather."

Max winked at Piper as he walked to the side door and called out to his team. "Everyone come inside, but take your shoes off at the door. After we eat, we've got some work to do."

Not a single player protested as they filed into the

house, grinning at Piper and Mrs. Anderson, several of them thanking the ladies for making them supper.

Piper was never so happy to see forty teenagers in her life. She just wondered if she had enough to keep them busy.

Chapter Six

"Thanks for all your help," Max called out to the last group of teenagers getting into a car. "See you tomorrow at the game."

Darkness had fallen and Third Street was full of the glow of lights from the houses all around the bed-and-breakfast. For a second, Max just stood and soaked up the simplicity of his hometown. There had been a time in his life when the quiet streets and lack of nightlife had bored him. But now, after seeing all the "excitement" the world had to offer, he could finally appreciate the quiet stability of Timber Falls.

Stepping back into the foyer, he closed and locked the front door. The lights were still on in the dining room and he could hear the faint tinkling sounds of silverware.

Max flipped off the foyer lights and walked into the dining room.

Piper was at the built-in hutch, polishing the silverware before putting it in one of the drawers. She glanced up when Max entered. "Your team did such a great job getting all my chores done, I had to make myself look busy, so I decided to polish the silverware." She tried to hide a sheepish smile. "I never polish the silverware."

Max laughed and went to her side to pick up a rag to help her finish. "Did they do an okay job?"

"Better than okay. There was so much help, we got things done I had only dreamed of accomplishing, like washing windows, wiping down floorboards and flipping the mattresses." Piper leaned against the hutch. "All I had to do was walk around and supervise."

"They were happy to help," he said. "I had to force them to go home."

Max had been helping with the outside work. The lawn was mowed, the flower beds were weeded and the gutters were cleaned. He had caught sight of Piper only once or twice all evening, but she was always bringing a smile to someone's face when he saw her. The team loved her—everyone loved her. She was still the town sweetheart.

"I'll happily feed your team a spaghetti dinner any night of the week if it means I can get that kind of help." She put her piece of silverware back into the drawer.

"Thanks, again, for putting the meal together so quickly. I wouldn't have suggested it if I had known you and Mrs. Anderson were so busy."

She waved aside his comment with her rag. "I was happy to do it."

Max wiped down a spoon and held it up to see his reflection. "I actually have another favor to ask."

Piper grabbed a fork and raised her eyebrows. "I'm almost afraid to ask what it is. Do you need me to feed all the fans at the game tomorrow night?"

"No." He grinned and put the spoon in the drawer

and then picked up another one. "I was approached by Mrs. Tanner today after practice."

"Mrs. Tanner?" Piper stopped polishing her fork. "Is she still teaching home economics?"

"Apparently." Max shrugged, still amazed to see their old teacher with so much energy. Mrs. Tanner had been old when they had been in school. Now, she seemed ancient. "But she corrected me when I called it home ec. Now it's called home and consumer sciences class."

"Fancy," Piper said with a dimpled smile. "What did she want?"

"She's still in charge of the homecoming committee and made a special request—for the both of us."

Piper slowly began to polish the fork again. "What kind of special request?"

"It seems the homecoming king and queen from last year are unable to attend the coronation this year to crown the new king and queen." Max watched Piper's reaction closely. "Mrs. Tanner needs alumni from a former year to stand in their place and she remembered that we were homecoming royalty. She asked if we'd be willing to crown the new king and queen and then stay at the dance afterward to help chaperone."

Piper set down the fork and didn't pick up another. She also didn't meet Max's gaze. "I don't know. It's on a Friday night, isn't it? I'll have my hands full with our guests."

"It's not for a couple more weeks, and if you're worried about your work here, I can always hire someone to come in and help Mrs. Anderson that evening." He hadn't been thrilled with the invitation to attend homecoming, but it would be the right thing to do—and if Piper was willing to be there, it might even be fun.

"I'm not sure." Piper wrinkled her nose. "I'd feel kind of silly being onstage again—especially looking like this." She pointed to her stomach.

"You're adorable." And he meant it. He'd never seen anyone look as good as she did while pregnant.

Her cheeks filled with color. "Maybe in a pair of overalls—but in an evening gown? I don't even own one. Do they make them for pregnant women?"

Max shrugged. How was he supposed to know?

"No matter what you wear, I'm sure you'll look great." He smiled. "If you don't want to do it for yourself, do it for good ol' Timber Falls High." He set down the spoon he'd been holding. "And, if that's not enough incentive, would you do it for me? A favor? I don't want to be up there all by myself."

She put her hand on her stomach in a gesture he was noticing more and more—as if the baby somehow brought her comfort. "Okay," she sighed. "I'll do it." She picked up a fork and pointed it at him. "But if I look ridiculous in a gown, I'm blaming you."

He laughed. "Piper, I don't think you could look ridiculous in anything." It had been a week since he'd returned to town, but their old comradery was starting to return. He always knew he missed her, but it wasn't until she was in his life again, every day, that he realized how much his life had lacked without her friendship.

"As long as you don't wear a plastic garbage bag to homecoming, I think you'll be safe."

She rolled her eyes. "You're impossible, Max Evans. How's a girl supposed to trust anything you say?"

She paused, her entire demeanor turning sober. "I'm sorry—that didn't come out right."

Max stood up straighter, her words, though spoken in jest, were like a splash of cold water on the moment. He tried to brush it off. "It's okay, Piper. I know what you meant."

She nodded and put the last fork back into the drawer. "I should probably get to sleep. It'll be a long weekend."

Max handed her his rag. "Same here. First home game tomorrow."

An awkward silence soon filled the space where their laughter and joking had just resided.

And despite Piper apologizing, and Max telling her it was okay, he realized that no matter how many good memories returned, they would never overshadow the bad ones. And it was the bad ones that had ultimately defined their relationship.

The announcer's voice blared from the small radio on the windowsill in the kitchen where Mrs. Anderson stood making buttermilk biscuits for tomorrow's breakfast. Piper sat nearby, in the little alcove office under the back stairs, trying hard to focus on the work she was doing for a baby shower that had just been scheduled at the bed-and-breakfast. It was for Kate Dawson, the pastor's wife, who was expecting a baby around the same time as Piper. The party would be in seven weeks, but there were several things that needed to be arranged now.

"It sounds like the fans are excited for the game," Mrs. Anderson called to Piper, wiping flour on her apron. "I can hear the pep band in the background and the cheers from the crowd are almost drowning out the announcer."

Piper finished the email she was working on and listened to the radio for a couple seconds. A rush of nostalgic emotions filled her chest at the familiar sound of a Friday night football game. How many Lumberjacks games had she watched over the years? She hadn't been back to the field since graduating high school and had never had the desire to go—until now. Before, football games only brought back bad memories. But now that Max was home and there had been some semblance of reconciliation between them, the negative feelings didn't resurface.

Instead, she suddenly missed it all. The cheering fans, the bright lights, the fearless players and the smell of popcorn on the cool breeze.

Leaving the little alcove, Piper walked over to Mrs. Anderson and leaned against the counter. The house was full of guests and the anticipation for the fun weekend ahead was almost palpable. Even now, a group who had come in for the arts and crafts festival were in the parlor laughing and playing a game. Another group was in the dining room visiting. Mrs. Anderson had kept busy refilling the snacks and beverages table all evening.

"It sounds like everyone's having a good time," Piper said.

"Everyone but you."

Piper looked up quickly. "What are you talking about? I'm having fun."

"When?" she asked, her hands busy rolling out the dough.

"Just last weekend I was at my class reunion."

Mrs. Anderson stopped rolling the dough and lifted an eyebrow. "You were on the planning committee and were technically working that evening. When was the last time you actually did something just for the fun of it?"

Piper opened her mouth to counter the accusation—but she couldn't think of a single thing that she'd done for months that didn't involve the bed-and-breakfast, her business or some sort of volunteer activity.

"I'm not saying that working hard is bad." Mrs. Anderson set down the rolling pin and picked up the biscuit cutter. "I'm just saying that you should do something for yourself once in a while."

"I haven't had the luxury."

"I know. But things have settled down a little and now would be the time—especially before the baby arrives."

Piper shrugged. "What would I do for fun?"

Mrs. Anderson started to cut out the biscuits and lay them on a baking sheet. "Why not take yourself to the football game?"

The radio wasn't too loud, but it was loud enough for Piper to follow all the action. The kickoff was underway as she watched Mrs. Anderson work.

"I'd feel silly going to the game by myself."

"Oh, you won't be by yourself," she chided. "You'll know almost everyone in the stands."

"You know what I mean."

Mrs. Anderson cut out another biscuit. "What about Liv? What is she doing this weekend? Maybe she'll go with you." The oven timer went off and she put a mitt on her hand and took out the first batch of biscuits. The delicious aroma wafted around Piper. "I'd go, but

I have a few things I need to get done before tomorrow morning."

Piper crossed her arms, her pulse accelerated at the thought of returning to the Timber Falls High School football field. Would Liv want to go with her? When was the last time she did something for fun with her friend? Every time they saw each other, it was all work, work, work.

"Give her a call," Mrs. Anderson said. "It can't hurt to ask her."

"Okay." Piper finally nodded. She'd call Liv, though she didn't think her friend would be interested in going to the game. Liv hadn't enjoyed football even in high school. "If she's not available, I'll just find a good book to read." It had been a long time since she'd read something for pleasure and her to-be-read pile was as tall as her.

Piper found her phone near her computer in the alcove and called Liv.

"Hey, Piper," Liv said. "I just got your email with all the information for the baby shower."

"Hi, Liv." Piper couldn't sit, so she paced back into the kitchen. The thought of going to the game was more and more appealing, especially with the sounds of the game echoing through the room from the radio.

They talked for a couple of minutes about the email, but then Piper said suddenly, "I didn't call about the email—I'm actually calling to see if you'd like to go to the football game with me."

There was a pause on the other end of the line, and then Liv finally said, "The high school game?"

"Yes. Mrs. Anderson has it playing on the radio and

it made me a little nostalgic. I thought it might be fun to go." She held her breath, wondering what Liv would say.

"I'm already in my pajamas for the night."

The disappointment was heavy and swift. Piper sat down in her chair, trying to hide the weight of it from her voice. "Yeah, I wasn't even sure if you'd be interest—"

"I didn't say I wasn't interested, just that I've already settled in for the night." She paused. "But, if you'd really like to go, I can be ready in a couple minutes and meet you up at the parking lot."

"I wouldn't want you to go to too much trouble—"

"Piper?"

"Yeah."

"When was the last time you asked me to hang out with you?"

Guilt washed over Piper. "It's been a while."

"Exactly. I'm not about to turn you down now. I'll see you up at the high school parking lot in about ten minutes. I'll be the one with the big smile on my face."

Piper grinned. "Thanks, Liv."

They hung up and Piper sat for a minute, thanking God for her friends.

"Well?" Mrs. Anderson asked. "What did Liv have to say?"

"She said she'll meet me there."

Mrs. Anderson's eyes lit up and she smiled. "What are you waiting for?"

Piper stood and went to Mrs. Anderson. She gave her a quick side hug. "Thank you."

And then she went to her room and changed into some black leggings, a white shirt, a long, gray cardigan and a dark green sweater scarf. She pulled warm socks onto her feet and put on her tall brown boots. There was no time to do anything special with her hair, so she put it up in a messy bun and glanced in the mirror. Her rounded tummy was the first thing that caught her eye. She placed her hands there and smiled when the baby moved under her fingers.

Her child was never far from her thoughts, though she'd had precious little time to really dwell on her pregnancy since Nick's death. With the opening of the bed-and-breakfast, she'd felt herself taking a deep breath for the first time in months, but the creditors were not far from her thoughts. Money from the sale of the bed-and-breakfast had helped, but she still wasn't debt-free. She didn't think she could really relax until the last creditor was paid, which, if all went well with the big wedding in November, and a few of the smaller events she was coordinating, would be by Thanksgiving, just a month before the baby was born.

"If we can just hold on until then," she whispered to her unborn child, "we'll have a fresh start and I can focus all my attention on finding a place to make our very own."

It felt daunting, the idea of starting over, but also freeing.

In less than five minutes, Piper pulled into the high school parking lot. It was close enough she could have walked, but she didn't want to be out walking alone at night.

The large lights from the field drew her attention as she stepped out of her car. A roar filled the air and a quick glimpse at the scoreboard told Piper the Timber Falls Lumberjacks had just made a touchdown. It was now 13-0 and not even halftime. Even without Tad, it looked like the Lumberjacks were a strong team.

"Hi, Piper!" Liv stepped out of her car not too far away. She looked great in her skinny jeans and over-size cowl-necked sweater. If Piper hadn't talked to her ten minutes ago and heard she was ready for bed, she would have never believed it.

"Hey, Liv." Piper grabbed a checkered flannel blanket from the passenger seat and closed the door. She met Liv near the ticket gate. "Thanks for coming on such short notice."

"And miss all this?" Liv smiled. "I'm happy to be here. Thanks for the invitation."

They paid for their admittance, had their hands stamped with the Lumberjacks logo, and entered the stadium.

All the sights and sounds hit Piper at the same moment and she took a deep inhale of popcorn-scented air.

The Lumberjacks kicked a field goal, making the score 14-0, and the crowd went wild.

"Did Max ask you to come?" Liv asked as they walked up to the chain-link fence that circled the football field.

There were hundreds of people filling the tall bleachers, lining the paved path around the perimeter of the field and mingling outside the snack shop. Everywhere Piper looked, she saw people she knew, and several smiled a greeting at her.

"Max mentioned there was a home game," Piper said, "but he didn't ask me if I wanted to be here."

"That's a bummer." Liv's smile fell.

"Why?" Piper frowned.

"I thought that's why we were here, because of Max."

Just then, Piper's gaze landed on Max. He stood on the sideline with the Lumberjacks, clapping and patting the offensive linemen on the shoulders as they came off the field. He looked up at that same moment and caught sight of Piper.

They were too far away to say anything to each other, but the look of pleasure on Max's face at seeing her was all the communication she needed.

A flutter of nervous butterflies filled her stomach and when he smiled at her, she smiled back.

If she was honest with herself, they were there because of Max. She had wanted to see him on the field again—and it was just as wonderful as it had always been.

"It looks as if he's happy to see you." Liv leaned her arms on the top of the fence. "At least that's something."

Max's attention was torn back to his team as his defensive line went into position to defend their goal.

A cool wind turned the tip of Piper's nose cold, but the warmth of Max's smile, coupled with the happy memories that had returned to her when she stepped into the stadium, were enough to make her realize she wouldn't need her blanket, after all.

"I think he's just happy to be back on the football field," Piper said, not willing to accept that Max's happiness was due to her presence alone.

She couldn't let herself believe Max cared that much.

Chapter Seven

The energy from winning the game followed Max as he left the front doors of Timber Falls High and entered the parking lot. Just like when he was in high school, there were dozens of people waiting for the players. Some were friends, some were parents and others were girlfriends waiting on their boyfriends.

A part of Max had hoped Piper would be there, waiting for him like she used to. He'd caught a glimpse of her at the start of the second quarter and his heart had done a little flip. When she smiled back at him, he thought he might need to sit down, his legs were so weak from the unexpected sight of her.

She had come. Just like when they were teenagers. Knowing she was there to cheer him on had given him an extra boost of confidence.

He'd soon lost track of her in the sea of fans and he had forced himself to focus on the game, instead of searching the bleachers for another glimpse of her every chance he could get.

Now, as he scanned the group waiting outside the school, disappointment weighed him down—but then he remembered he was going back to the house where she lived. He hoped and prayed she would still be awake so they could talk. He had always wanted to know her thoughts after the games he had played and had missed her perspective all these years. But it was getting late and he doubted she'd be awake.

Several people tried to stop Max as he moved through the waiting crowd, and he suddenly realized a lot of them had been there hoping to get a chance to say hi to him. Some were old classmates from different grades, there were also friends of his parents, former teachers and even a few people he didn't know who wanted to meet him.

As quickly as he could, he maneuvered his way through the crowd and jumped into his Lexus. Thankfully, the bed-and-breakfast was only six blocks away and it didn't take him long to pull up to the house.

The place was packed for the weekend and there was no place to park in the small parking lot, so he pulled to a stop on the street in front.

Though the hour was late, almost all the lights were ablaze inside the Victorian home.

Max pulled his duffel bag out of the car and stopped for a minute to admire the house. It looked like one of those paintings with the soft light and cozy atmosphere. He still marveled that Piper could envision the potential for the house when she was a child, even when it was dilapidated and in disrepair. He couldn't imagine how much work it had taken for her to bring it back to its original glory.

He walked toward the house and almost passed Piper sitting on one of the white rocking chairs on the wraparound porch.

There were no lights on the porch and only the gentle glow from inside illuminated her.

"Hey," he said, his pulse ticking a little higher.

"Good game tonight."

"Thanks." Max set down his duffel bag and walked to the chair next to her. "Mind if I join you?"

She shook her head. "Of course not."

The rocker squeaked in protest as he sat, but it was a welcome sound after the loud cheering on the field.

Piper wore a red-and-black-checkered blanket over her shoulders as she looked out at the dark yard. In her hand was a steaming cup, and upon sitting closer to her, he could smell the faint hint of hot chocolate.

He had forgotten how much she liked hot chocolate.

"What are you doing out here?" he asked. "I thought you'd be in bed by now."

"Liv came here after the game for some hot cocoa." She lifted the mug. "The first cup was for me but this one is for the baby." She smiled and took another sip. "Liv just left and I thought I'd sit out here a little longer. All the excitement of the game, and the caffeine from the cocoa, will prevent me from falling asleep. Besides," she nodded toward the house, "I don't think that group of ladies is going to be going to bed anytime soon."

The light from the parlor illuminated one side of her face, highlighting her creamy skin and high cheekbones.

When she turned and met his gaze, her eyes made him catch his breath and he couldn't hide his pleasure at seeing her—now or at the game. "I was happy you came tonight," he said, his voice revealing the depth of his feelings. "The team played well."

"Even without Tad."

"Yeah." He let out a long sigh. "He refuses to answer my calls or return my texts. My mom asked me to come over for lunch after church on Sunday to talk to him."

"Are you going?"

Max nodded. "Yeah, but I don't think he'll talk."

She reached out with her free hand and laid it on his arm. "Just keep trying. Don't give up. You'll get through to him."

He looked down at her long slender fingers, and wanted to put his hand over hers, but knew if he did, she'd pull away. There were so many emotions churning in his mind and heart, and seeing her at the game tonight had made him realize how much he still wanted Piper to be a part of his life. For years, he thought his chances with her were dead, but over the past couple of weeks, a spark of hope had begun to burn again. He didn't want to make any more blunders. He wanted to regain her trust, but he couldn't do it all at once. He'd have to do it one day at a time.

She removed her hand and smiled again. "It was good to be back at the field tonight. Your defense is strong, though your offense needs a little work. I'm sure they were just off without Tad."

"You're right." He was thankful they were talking about a safe subject for now. "A lot of my guys depend on Tad too much. They get sloppy out there sometimes. We worked hard on our offensive line this week and I was happy to see they did a pretty decent job, considering."

"It's a good team, Max. I have a feeling you could take them all the way this year."

"If my brother gets his act together. We played a

weak team tonight. They're not all this easy to beat. We need Tad to take the team all the way to the championship game. I'd hate to see him mess things up like I did."

Piper was quiet for a long time. The muffled laughter from inside the house seeped onto the porch and the wind tousled the leaves on the elm trees around the property.

"I'm happy I went," Piper finally said. "It's been too long."

"There's something special about those Friday night lights, isn't there? I've played in all the major stadiums in America, but there's nothing quite like my own high school football field."

"Are you happy you came back?"

Max slowly nodded. There was so much on his heart tonight. How could he keep it all inside? "For more than one reason."

She didn't speak as she watched him.

"If I hadn't come back when I did," he said, "I don't know how long it would have taken me to get the courage to face you again." All those years he had thought it was easier just to avoid her. But now, sitting beside her, smelling the floral shampoo she used in her hair, admiring the curve of her cheeks, looking into her familiar eyes, he realized it had been far easier to return than he'd thought.

It had never been hard to be with Piper. The difficulty came when he'd been away from her.

But did he have it in him to stay? What would happen if it became hard again? Would he run, like he'd always done? He couldn't take that risk. Living with the guilt and shame of hurting Piper had nearly destroyed him. To do it a second time would surely be the end of him.

"Piper?"

She watched him, a question in her eyes.

His phone started to ring.

Piper's gaze dropped to his pocket. "Are you going to get that?"

The last thing he wanted was an interruption. "No." He pulled the phone out to turn off the ringer and saw his ex-girlfriend's name in big, bold letters.

Margo.

Piper glanced at the screen and Max's first instinct was to hide Margo's name from her.

He fumbled with the silence button and then shoved the phone back into his pocket, his palms sweating. What did Margo want? Had Piper seen her name?

"Don't you need to answer her?" Piper asked quietly, returning her gaze to the dark yard.

So she had seen it.

"No." Max shook his head. "I have nothing to say to her."

"Why do you think she's calling you?"

Was it his imagination, or did he hear jealousy in Piper's tone?

"I haven't spoken to Margo in months." He wanted to add that he didn't know why she was calling now, but he had a feeling she was calling on behalf of her father and his job offer.

"What do you think she wants?"

Max opened his mouth to tell her he had no idea— but it would be a lie, and he'd made a promise almost twenty years ago that he'd never lie to Piper. And he hadn't. Not even the night when it all went wrong. He'd been brutally honest about the party, the alcohol and the girl. But Piper hadn't given him a second chance then and he wondered, after all these years, if she would now.

"I'm sorry," she said, standing up. "It's none of my business."

Max also stood. "It's okay, Piper. We're friends. You can ask me about my life."

Her blanket fell and Max leaned over to pick it up for her.

"It's still none of my business." She took the blanket from him in her free hand and started to move around him.

Max touched her arm to stop her. "I want you to ask about my life. I have nothing to hide."

She was silent as she stood beside him, facing the opposite direction, but then she turned her head to look at Max. They were close enough that he could feel the warm breath from her lips. "If you don't have anything to hide, then why did you act that way when you saw her name on your phone?"

"The truth?" he asked her quietly.

She nodded.

"I didn't want you to think that she and I are still talking." He studied her features in the soft light. "Because the truth is, there's no one else I'd rather be talking to than you."

A heartbeat passed as Piper stared at Max, a dozen emotions passing over her face. "Why do you think she called?" she asked quietly for the third time.

"I'm not sure, though I might have an idea." He wouldn't keep the truth from her, no matter how it might affect their relationship, or what she might think. "Margo's father offered me a job."

She studied him in the muted light. "Where?"

"University of California at Mid-State, scouting for their football team."

"Will you take the job?"

There were so many things to consider, least of all was whether or not the Timber Falls school would offer him a regular position as the head coach—and even that wasn't enough of an incentive to stay in Timber Falls.

There was only one reason he'd stay and that was for Piper. Yet, even as the thought solidified, he knew it would be almost impossible for her to give him the opportunity to redeem himself—and even if she let him back into her life, he feared he could not be the man she needed.

Piper watched as several thoughts and emotions flickered across Max's face as he contemplated how to answer her question. Years of heartache twisted in her gut, and even though he had told her why Margo called, she still didn't trust that he was telling her the whole truth—and she despised herself for it. Why couldn't she trust him? Why must she assume the worst?

"I'm not sure if I'll take the job or not," he finally said. "There are a lot of unanswered questions in my life right now."

"Like what?" she asked, wanting desperately to understand.

He took her hand in his. "Like whether or not you'd ever give me another chance."

Instead of excitement, panic made Piper's heart race. When Max left ten years ago, she had been angry and disillusioned. Over the years, as she'd navigated a bad marriage, her heart had become even harder. As much as she wanted to return to a time when she was naive to heartbreak, she couldn't, and the idea of enduring it again felt like she was facing a bottomless pit. She despised the way she felt, and she despised the way her mind automatically assumed the worst—but she didn't know how to change. And right now, with a mountain of debt and a baby on the way, she didn't have the emotional or mental energy to try.

She pulled her hand away, hating herself for denying something she had wanted so badly as a young woman—but knowing she needed to protect herself and her child right now, at all costs. "I'm sorry, Max." She shook her head, but could not look at him. "I've been hurt a lot and my heart is still raw with grief." Tears swam in her eyes. "It's not even about what happened between us—not really." She finally got the courage to meet his gaze and saw the pain and anguish there. "Things between Nick and me were really bad, for a long time, and I'm afraid my heart has grown cynical to love." The thought that she might never trust Max—or anyone else again—gave her an icy chill up her spine.

"Is there nothing I can do to help change your mind?"

A tear escaped her eye and slid down her cheek. Piper dashed it away as she shook her head, her heart breaking all over again. "I wish there was, Max, but I think it's too late." She *knew* it was too late. Despite what he said about her on the night of the reunion, she *wasn't* the same person she had been ten years ago. Her heart had become calloused and bruised, beyond repair.

"Good night, Max." Piper forced herself to remember the promise she made to herself when Max walked back into her life. She would be friendly and professional, but she wouldn't get close to him again. There was too much at stake. She didn't need to know what decisions he had to make, or what kinds of offers he'd been given. None of it concerned her and she told herself it didn't matter. She and Max were leading two different lives. He owed her no explanation.

She walked to the door.

"Piper, wait." Max turned and half of his face was visible from the light, while the other half was shrouded in darkness. For a moment, she saw the young Max in his gaze. The best friend, the playmate and the confidant. "I'm sorry you're hurting and I'm sorry I was the cause of some of that pain." He took a tentative step toward her and stopped. "If I could, I would storm the castle and chase away the dragons for you."

Another tear slipped down her cheek. "I know you would."

He took another step toward her and she went into his embrace. He held her in his arms and simply comforted her.

She clung to him, remembering how many times he'd been there to offer his powerful embrace when life had been difficult growing up. On the day she'd gone to school so tired she could hardly see, because her father had been so drunk the night before that she had stayed awake to make sure he was breathing. On the anniversary of her mother's death each year, when Max would take her to the cemetery to bring flowers, because her father refused to go. When holidays and birthdays came around and her father was so ashamed he couldn't buy her gifts he stayed at the bar all day to avoid her.

Max had been there for her every single time, and

after he had left, there had been countless other times she wished he had still been there to hug her through the heartache. Like the day her dad had died from a heart attack a year after high school graduation, and the first of many weekends when Nick had chosen not to come home to her and didn't call or tell her where he'd been, or the night Nick had died and she had wept so deeply she'd been afraid for the unborn child she carried. Those were the times when she missed Max's hugs the most.

"Piper," Max whispered as he held her. "Even if you're not willing to give us a second chance, I want you to know something."

Her cheek lay against his chest and she could hear the steady beating of his heart against her ear, but she did not speak as she waited for him to continue.

"You will always be my best friend."

She closed her eyes as the tears ran freely down her cheeks. Maybe they should have never turned their friendship into a romance. If they hadn't, they could have spared each other so much pain.

It was a good thing he'd been offered a job by Margo's dad. Max needed to move on with his life and he needed to do it without any regret from his past holding him back. Maybe the reason for Max's return to Timber Falls and to the bed-and-breakfast was for both of them to have closure on this chapter of their life. To forgive each other and then to move on.

Piper took a steadying breath and she pulled away from Max's embrace. She tried to smile, but it was a wobbly effort. Despite what he said, they could never be best friends again. "I'm so thankful you have been a part of my life," she said as she looked up into his dark eyes. "But I think it would be best for both of us if we moved on with our lives. We can never go back." She had to stop and collect her emotions in case they clogged her throat. "Good night, Max."

She walked into the house and left him on the porch. As she passed through the dining room full of strangers laughing and having a good time, she had to remember that this bed-and-breakfast was just a stopping-over place for Max Evans. He was there for a season—just one.

They had one chance to heal their past so both of them could move forward without any more regrets.

That's what she would choose to focus on.

Chapter Eight

Piper turned off the engine of her car and sat in the parking lot of Timber Falls High, trying to get up the nerve to walk into the school in her evening gown. She was running a little late, but she couldn't force herself to get out of the car. The coronation was to begin at seven and she was supposed to meet Max in the hallway outside the gymnasium at quarter to the hour. It was that time right now.

With a deep breath to steady her shaking hands, she stepped out of the car. The purplish-blue-colored chiffon fabric slid down her smooth legs and pooled around her ankles. The top of the gown was made of lace, with long sleeves, and she wore heels for the first time in months. Mrs. Anderson and Liv had helped pin up her hair in a loose chignon at the nape of her neck, and Liv had loaned her a pair of simple diamond earrings. They had raved about her appearance as Piper had studied herself in the mirror, telling her how her eyes matched the color of the gown. She couldn't deny that the gown was gorgeous, or that it fit her perfectly, but she still felt a bit silly wearing something so elegant and refined when she was six months pregnant.

The parking lot was full of teenagers arriving at the dance in their own gowns and rented tuxedos, which was a small consolation to Piper. At least she wasn't the only one walking into the school dressed so elaborately—though she was the only one pregnant. She felt like a dumpy potato in a field of sunflowers.

"Hello, Mrs. Connelly!" One of the girls from Timber Falls Community Church was entering the school. Piper had known her for years. "You look pretty," she said.

"Thank you." Piper smiled. "So do you."

A young man opened the door for Piper to walk into the school. The entrance was crowded with several students. A line had formed as they waited to pay for their admittance.

Piper bypassed all the teenagers, saying hello here and there as she recognized some of the students, and went to the front of the line. The activities director waved her along, knowing she was needed in the gymnasium.

A set of doors led into the mezzanine, with the gymnasium floor down below. The room was decorated like a park, complete with streetlamps, a winding path and park benches. A stage stood at one end of the room where a DJ played music. Students were already mingling in the gym, though no one was dancing yet. That would come later, after the coronation.

Piper walked to the set of steps that led to the hallway where Max said he'd be waiting for her outside his office. He had wanted to come home and pick her up, but the team had practiced after school and then Max had to attend a mandatory coaches meeting. Piper had insisted she could come herself.

Almost a month had passed since they had stood on the front porch and she had told him it was too late for a second chance. Since then, Max had been kind—but he had kept his distance, interacting with her only when it was necessary. During the day, he worked on projects around the house, mostly outside, and after three o'clock, he went to the football field for practice. He didn't come back to the bed-and-breakfast until well into the evening and went right up to his apartment. On the weekends, he spent time at his mom's working on odd projects she had around her house.

Tonight would be the first time they would have to be in each other's company for an extended period of time and she wasn't sure how it would go. Would it be awkward?

Did it have to be?

Piper held the handrail with one hand and pulled up the hem of her long skirt with the other. She took the stairs carefully, trying to see past her tummy to make sure she didn't fall. When she set her foot on the last step, she glanced up and found Max standing in the hall watching her.

Her breath caught and she paused on the bottom step.

Max wore a dark gray suit which fit him to perfection. She remembered seeing him in a suit very much like it in a magazine one time at the grocery store when he had been dating Margo. His lean waist and muscular shoulders and arms were accentuated in the well-tailored clothes. His hair looked as if he'd run his hands through it a few times—but it was his dark brown eyes, which lit up when he saw her, that drew her attention.

"Piper." He shook his head in amazement and she knew the look of appreciation on his face was authentic. "You look beautiful."

Under Max's gaze, she *felt* beautiful, even though she was six months pregnant.

"Thank you." She admired his suit, knowing it must have cost a small fortune. "You look really nice, too."

He ran his hand down the lapel of his suit. "It's been a while since I had a reason to wear this."

"You should have a reason to wear it more often." The words slipped out of her mouth before she could stop them and warmth filled her cheeks. She rolled her eyes playfully and said, "What is it about a high school dance that makes people say awkward and uncomfortable things?"

Max's laughter filled the long hall. "You still look cute when you get embarrassed. Do you remember that time we were in speech class and you got hiccups in the middle of your persuasive speech?"

Piper had practiced her speech for days in advance, but when the hiccups suddenly attacked, she had asked the teacher if she could give her speech a different day. The teacher had thought she was trying to get out of her speech and had said she needed to give it, regardless of the hiccups. "I don't think I ever convinced the class to take up the tuba that day."

"You might have bombed the speech, but you looked adorable while doing it." His grin was wide. "I don't remember anyone else's persuasive speech but yours."

Piper put her hands up to her warm cheeks. "I'm so happy high school is over."

"It's definitely a lot more fun to be here on the other side of things, isn't it?" Max held out his elbow for her.

"Ready to go crown this year's homecoming king and queen?"

"Anything would be better than continuing this conversation." Piper wrapped her hand around his elbow, thankful to shift the focus off her.

Max led her into the gymnasium. The lights had been lowered and the DJ was playing a slow song as people trickled into the room. There was an air of discomfort as the teenagers stood around in their fancy clothes. Piper remembered how it felt to get over the initial shyness of seeing friends and classmates in a different situation, all dressed up in the gymnasium when they were used to seeing each other there in sweaty clothes during phys ed.

Tad entered with his girlfriend, Shelby, on his arm. He looked so much like Max had at his age, Piper had to look twice. The only difference between Max and Tad was that Max wasn't arrogant and had never had a haughty attitude like Tad did. Tad carried himself with his chin high, as if he was the most important thing that had ever happened to Timber Falls High.

When Max caught sight of his brother, he waved. Shelby returned the wave, but Tad turned away without acknowledging Max.

Piper glanced up at Max and saw the pain in his expression. But when he saw she was watching him, he smiled and winked at her. "I won't give up," he said.

Mrs. Tanner, the home economics teacher, was there, fussing and fretting. Her thin hair looked as if she'd recently had it styled, the grayish-purple strands were locked tight in a weblike structure and her old-fashioned black-rimmed glasses were smudged. She wore a dress that looked as old as her. "Oh, good," she said when she saw Max and Piper approach the stage. "You made it."

Several hundred students mingled in the gymnasium. The smell of perfume and cologne made Piper's stomach turn, but she forced herself to ignore the nausea and, instead, focused on the faces of the teenagers gathered.

Memories of her and Max's homecoming filled her with a mixture of feelings and she couldn't help but wonder how many of these kids were hiding behind their smiles. How many were struggling in school? At home? In their relationships? Tonight was a fun night, but for some of the kids—like it had been for Piper—real life would be waiting for them at the stroke of midnight. She hoped and prayed that they had friends like Max who would be there to offer strength and comfort on the especially hard days.

She glanced at Max and found him listening to Mrs. Tanner ramble on about homecomings in the past. The old teacher looked at Piper and said, "Are you ready?"

"As ready as I'll ever be."

A microphone stood in the center of the stage and Mrs. Tanner walked up to it. She tapped it and blew into it, making the sounds echo through the large room. "Check, one, two, check, one, two," she said and then looked at the DJ and said, "Is this on?"

He winced and put his hand up to the headphones he was wearing and nodded emphatically.

"Good," she said. She cleared her throat and the sound ricocheted off the walls of the gymnasium. "Welcome to Timber Falls Homecoming Dance."

She paused, probably expecting applause, but the students just stared at her.

"Could the homecoming royalty court please come to the stage?" Mrs. Tanner read off the names of the five boys and five girls who had the most votes in the senior class. Tad and Shelby were among the names listed. Three other boys were members of the football team, but Piper didn't recognize the fifth boy.

When everyone was onstage, Mrs. Tanner said into the microphone, "Congratulations to this year's homecoming royalty!"

The crowd clapped this time and the kids onstage grinned.

Max stood beside Piper at the rear of the stage. He glanced at her and she smiled at him. It felt like just yesterday that they were standing on this stage, waiting to hear if they'd been elected king and queen to represent the school during homecoming week.

"And to crown this year's king and queen, we have two special guests," Mrs. Tanner continued, excitement in her voice. "Our very own alumnus Max Evans!" She stopped and allowed the crowd to applaud again. But then her gaze landed on Piper and she said, "Oh, yes, and Piper Pierson Connelly."

Max took Piper's hand and they stepped into the center of the stage to wave at the group.

"Max and Piper were crowned the king and queen of their senior homecoming," Mrs. Tanner said, "and have agreed to stand in for last year's couple who could not be with us this year."

After the cheering subsided, they stepped back. An assistant handed Piper a tiara and a robe for the queen and to Max, they gave a crown and a scepter for the king.

"And now, the moment we've all been waiting for,"

Mrs. Tanner said, pausing dramatically. "This year's king and queen are Tad Evans and Shelby Raskins!"

The room erupted in more cheers and Max grinned as he stepped forward to place the crown on his brother's head.

"Congrats," Max said to Tad and gave him a hug.

Piper also moved forward and smiled at Shelby. "Congratulations," she said, placing the tiara on her blond curls.

Shelby was crying and shaking, and saying over and over, "Thank you!"

It brought more memories back to Piper and she hugged the girl before placing the robe over her shoulders. "You look beautiful," she said to the girl. "Never forget this moment."

Piper and Max stood back and let the spotlight fall on Tad and Shelby.

"Crazy how fast time goes by," Max said quietly next to Piper. "If only we could go back and start over."

She didn't respond, because there was nothing she could say.

It had been a long day for Max and the evening started to wear on. The music the DJ was playing was foreign to his ears, the dances the kids were doing looked downright odd, and he was certain he'd never get used to so many of them with phones in their faces, even though they were standing in a group of their friends.

Piper stood on the other side of the gymnasium with one of the math teachers who was also the varsity basketball coach, a young, confident man who seemed quite taken with the dark-haired beauty. She was laughing at something he said and Max couldn't stop himself from feeling a tinge of jealousy. He wished Piper could be as carefree and comfortable with him. She was always on guard, even in their most lighthearted exchanges, as if she was afraid he would crush her spirit at any moment.

He hated feeling like a villain in her life. Hated even more that he was the only person to blame. The night they stood on the porch, and he had held her in his arms, his heart had pounded so hard he was certain she could feel it against her cheek. When he had asked her if she'd give him a second chance, and she said no, he knew she meant it.

So, he'd done the only thing he could, and gave both of them space. He kept to himself when he was at the bed-and-breakfast, tried to stay busy with the to-do list Mrs. Anderson had created and avoided meals with the ladies. He spent some much-needed time at his mom's, though Tad was rarely ever home and when he was, he ignored Max's attempts at working things out.

As the days turned to weeks, Max realized it would be impossible to stay in Timber Falls without having Piper in his life. His only option was to finish out the football season and then find another job. His best opportunity at the moment was to accept Tom Sutton's offer to be a scout for the University of California at Mid-State, but he didn't have to commit to the job now. He had time to focus on the Timber Falls Lumberjacks and to use whatever time he had left with Piper to rebuild their friendship so that, if nothing else, they could part as friends.

He did know that he would hold on to the bed-and-breakfast for as long as it took for Piper to save the money to buy it back from him. He'd keep her and Mrs. Anderson employed and let them manage it while he went on with his life.

But the very thought of leaving Piper gave him physical pain.

Shelby was on the dance floor with a group of her friends, making a video of some kind, but a quick glance around the gym told Max that Tad wasn't there. A sinking feeling hit Max in his gut and he walked to the doors leading to the lobby outside the gymnasium. Maybe Tad had just gone to the men's room, or maybe he was standing outside to get some fresh air.

But Max couldn't shake the memory of seeing his brother smoking that vape pen outside the theater. He just hoped his brother wasn't making a stupid choice again.

Max almost didn't want to find out—but the feeling propelled him to open the door to the outside and poke his head out to see if anything was amiss.

The evening was warmer than usual for early October and the sky was clear, allowing the stars to sparkle vibrantly overhead. Max stood for a moment at the open door, allowing his eyes to adjust to the dark when he saw two people standing together near the corner of the school. A girl was giggling and the sound of a deep voice was teasing and flirting.

Max would have gone back into the school to give them privacy, but as a chaperone, he needed to make sure all the students were inside and accounted for. Once they left the school grounds, they were free to do whatever they wanted, but while on the school property, they had to stick to the dance.

He started to move away from the door to tell the

couple to come back inside when Piper appeared behind him. "Everything okay?" she asked quietly.

Max nodded. "Just checking on things." He motioned toward the couple. "I was just going to tell them to come back to the dance."

"Okay." Piper smiled. "I'll wait for you and hold the door open. I think it locks from the outside when it's closed."

"Thanks." He hadn't even thought of that.

Max left her at the door and approached the couple. They were locked in a passionate embrace, so Max cleared his throat to warn them that he was near.

"Everyone needs to stay inside the school," he said.

The couple broke apart like they'd been caught doing something inappropriate—and that's when Max recognized his brother—but he didn't know the girl. She was a lot younger than Tad, and when she saw who Max was, she bolted for the school.

"Don't go, Brenna," Tad yelled after her, but when she didn't stop, Tad punched the brick building with his fist and then turned to Max. "What's your problem? Are you determined to ruin all my fun? Get your own life."

Tad pushed past Max, but Max wouldn't let him go this time. He grabbed Tad's arm, his anger rising.

"I'm not about to let you ruin your life, Tad. You have more going for you than all those kids in that gymnasium combined."

"Give me a break." Tad stopped and turned on Max. "How am I ruining my life by messing around with that girl?"

"How old is she?"

"Who knows? I don't even know her last name."

Max had to take a second to compose himself, afraid

his anger would make him lose the ability to talk rationally with his little brother. "She's probably a freshman, right?" Max asked.

Tad shrugged, but Max could see in his brother's eyes that he'd been right.

"And you turned eighteen a couple months ago. If her parents want to make an issue of it, you could get in a lot of trouble." Max tried to calm himself as he breathed heavily. "Not to mention that you have a girlfriend in that gym who thinks you're a pretty special guy and it would destroy her to know you're fooling around with someone else."

"Just like it destroyed Piper?" Tad asked with daggers in his voice.

Max inhaled a breath, feeling like his brother had just punched him.

Piper still stood at the open door and Max knew she could hear everything they said—but even if she couldn't, he would still say what needed to be said.

"My biggest regret in life was hurting her. If I could change one thing, that would be it."

"*That* is what you would change?" Tad asked, shaking his head in disgust. "What about abandoning Mom and me when we needed you most?"

"What?"

"You heard me." Tad's voice broke, but his shoulders were still tight with anger. "When dad died, it was just Mom and me. You didn't even bother to come home for Christmas or call on my birthday." Tad wiped at his face and Max wondered if he was crying. It was hard to see in the dark.

Guilt stabbed Max in the chest and he took a step toward his brother. "Tad—"

"Don't," Tad said, taking a step back. "You didn't care about anything but yourself. You had dozens of opportunities to make better choices, but you didn't. After you hurt Piper, you continued to hurt other people you loved—including me. So don't tell me you'd go back and make different choices. If given the opportunity, you'd do it all over again, and you wouldn't care who you hurt in the process."

"That's not true." But was it? Hadn't Max continued to hurt one person after the other? It wasn't until he was washed up in the NFL that he came back to Timber Falls to make amends. What would have happened if his career had been a success? Would he have continued to be selfish and self-serving?

"Keep lying to yourself, Max," Tad said, "but don't pretend you're better than me when you know you're not."

"I'm not better than you." Max knew he had made some bad mistakes, but he thanked God he was on a different path now. Maybe he couldn't go back and start over, but at least he could start from here and make a difference now. "I know I failed, but that's why I want you to listen to me and not make the same mistakes I made. You have the opportunity to do what I can't—live without regrets."

Tad's body was rigid as he listened and Max wondered what, if anything, was getting through to him.

"I'm sorry I wasn't there for you and Mom. I'm sorry I bailed on Timber Falls and all the people who matter to me. But you still have your life ahead of you. Be the man Mom and Dad taught you to be." Max's shoulders sagged. "Don't be like me."

"I don't have to listen to this." Tad stormed into the school, breezing past Piper on his way inside.

Max slowly walked to Piper. Even though it was dark, he could see the pain in her face reflected off the lights from inside.

"I'm sorry, Max," she whispered.

Max shook his head. He was failing with his brother and didn't know how to get through to him. Part of him just wanted to throw his hands up and let Tad live his own life. It would be a whole lot easier to walk away from his brother—but wasn't that what Tad had just accused Max of doing all along? Walking away? Giving up? Doing what was best for Max, regardless of what it meant for everyone else?

"Everything he said about me was true." Max wasn't looking for Piper's sympathy, but she offered it to him anyway.

"Maybe that was who you used to be," she said, "but it doesn't have to be who you are anymore. Anyone can change."

If he had really changed, and she saw it, would she give him another chance? Would Tad? "But even if I've changed," he asked softly, "how can I fix years of heartbreak and then convince the people I've hurt that I won't hurt them again?" He reached out—tentatively, afraid she'd pull away—and ran his thumb over the curve of her cheek. This wasn't about Tad anymore. "How can I have a second chance?"

She studied him under the starlight, sadness weighing down her mouth. She put her hand over his and lowered it away from her face. "Sometimes it's too late for a second chance, so you make your apologies and then move on, hoping for closure."

Closure. Was that what she truly wanted? He'd asked her twice now, but she had given him the same answer both times.

It was too late for them.

She let go of his hand and left him to return to the dance.

Max had no other choice. He couldn't stay and watch Piper's life from a distance. Once the season was over, he would move on from Timber Falls. It seemed the only option.

Until then, he'd have to settle for friendship and nothing more.

Chapter Nine

Clouds gathered over Piper as she walked out of the Family Medical Center, her hand on her swollen stomach. She was almost seven months along, only nine weeks until her due date, but the news she'd just been given at her routine prenatal appointment left her trembling.

"Hi, Piper!" A familiar voice pulled Piper from her scary thoughts and she found her friend Joy Asher stepping out of a large conversion van in the parking lot.

As Joy went around the van and opened the side door, Piper walked toward her. If anyone could understand Piper's worry, it would be Joy. Even though Joy was a couple years younger than Piper, she was the mother of six children. Three boys she and her husband, Chase, had adopted, a set of four-year-old twin girls, and a little baby boy who had been born that spring. Joy removed the baby's car seat from its base in the van and grabbed her diaper bag before closing the door and turning her attention to Piper.

"Just little Shepherd today?" Piper asked as she

peeked under the blanket covering him from the cool October air. "Is everything alright?"

"Everything is great. We're just here for Shep's sixth-month well-baby check." Joy smiled and met Piper's gaze, but then her smile faded and she frowned. "Is everything okay with you?"

Joy was a friend from church, but more than that, she and her husband managed the Asher Family Foundation, which existed to help widows and orphans in Timber Falls. They had donated a significant amount of money to help offset the cost of Nick's funeral and had been there every moment they could spare to help finish the bed-and-breakfast. Joy's friendship had always meant a great deal to Piper and she thanked God now that she had crossed Joy's path today of all days.

Piper shook her head and she had to fight the fear trying to close her throat. "Dr. Meeker just told me she's concerned that my body might be preparing for labor far too early. She wants me to stay off my feet as much as possible and come in next week for another appointment."

"Bed rest?" Joy asked, concern in her voice.

"No." Piper was quick to shake her head. "Not bed rest, but she said no housework or exercising, or anything that will have me up and about for more than ten or fifteen minutes. She'll check me again next week to see if things have progressed and let me know if I need to continue resting or can go back to my regular work."

Joy nodded. "I'm sorry, Piper. I had to do the same with the twins' pregnancy. I know you're concerned because you have a lot on your plate already." She put her free hand on Piper's arm. "I'm sure if you explain the situation to Mrs. Anderson and Max, they'll find ways to help. And I'll do what I can to help, too."

With six children and a busy foundation to run, Piper would never dream of asking Joy for help. It would be hard enough to ask Mrs. Anderson to pick up her extra work—impossible, really.

"Thank you," Piper said to Joy. "I'm sure things will work out."

But, even though she sounded positive and confident, she didn't feel that way. Not only did she have full occupancy this weekend, but she also had Kate Dawson's baby shower to organize and host at the bed-and-breakfast on Sunday afternoon, not to mention all the details she was still coordinating for Carrie Custer's wedding, which was only four short weeks away.

"I have to run," Joy said to Piper, "but I'll be praying for you. And, please, do not hesitate to call on me for help. If I can't do what's needed, I have a whole list of volunteers who are ready and willing to lend a hand if I simply let them know."

Piper smiled and nodded, but Joy looked at her with a serious face. "I'm not kidding, Piper. Don't be embarrassed or shy to call me for help. My offer is genuine."

"I know." Piper gave her friend a quick hug and then got into her car.

The bed-and-breakfast was only four blocks away, but it looked like it might rain, and now that Piper was supposed to take it easy, she was happy she had driven instead of walked.

She sat in her car for a second, watching Joy walk into the clinic, and tried hard not to cry. The last thing she wanted was to jeopardize her pregnancy and put her baby at risk, but how was she going to stay off her feet for the next week—or even longer?

She fought the tears all the way home and was thankful it was Wednesday and they still had two days before their next guests would arrive. Mrs. Anderson had the morning off and she hoped Max was in his apartment. She needed some time alone to pull her emotions together and to make a plan before she told them what the doctor had said.

But when Piper pulled up to the bed-and-breakfast, Max was standing out by the mailboxes, chatting with the mailman. Piper put the car in Park and hoped to sneak into the house without Max noticing—but it was no use. He waved at her and then nodded goodbye at the mailman and started to walk toward Piper.

She took a couple steadying breaths. Maybe she could hold herself together long enough to be neighborly with Max and then get inside before her real emotions took hold.

Raindrops started to fall and the wind picked up, blowing colorful leaves off the trees. They twisted and twirled as they danced through the air. Piper stepped out of her car and Max instinctively put the mail over his head and rushed to Piper's side. He put his arm around her shoulders and led her into the back entrance of the bed-and-breakfast.

The entry was dark, since there were no windows in the back hall, but before the door closed, Max glanced down at Piper and his eyes filled with worry.

"What's wrong, Piper?"

She frowned and pushed aside his concern. "Don't worry about it."

"I am worried about it." He closed the back door

and flipped on the light switch. The entry wasn't very large and Max stood close to her. "I can tell something is wrong by the look on your face."

Piper was struggling to take a deep breath—whether it was from Max standing so close, or the confines of the entry or her own hormonal emotions, she wasn't sure, but she needed some space. She opened the door leading into the private living area and took off her jacket.

There was no use hiding the truth from Max. They knew each other so well—he could see she was upset and she knew he wouldn't let her be until she told him what was bothering her.

The wind picked up speed outside and the rain fell in earnest now. She shivered. "Would you like some hot cocoa?" she asked as she walked past the gas fireplace and flipped on the switch.

"I'd like for you to tell me what's wrong." Max stood by the door, the mail still in his hands. "I can tell something is bothering you."

Piper went into the kitchen and took the kettle off the back burner. She filled it with water and set it back on the stove to warm.

Max closed the door and followed her into the kitchen. He set the mail on the counter and then stood there, his arms crossed, and stared at her. "Talk to me, Piper."

She knew he'd overreact. She also knew she didn't want him to care that much. When Nick died, Piper had come to terms with doing this pregnancy on her own. Sure, she had the help of her friends and church family, but ultimately, she was going to stand on her own two feet and be a single parent.

As Max waited for her to tell him what was wrong, she instinctively knew he'd step up to the plate and help. Part of her longed for that help, but the other part wanted to keep him as far away as possible. The less involved he became in her life, the easier it would be to say goodbye.

She picked up the mail and started to leaf through it—until she saw the creditor's return address on an envelope. It was the big one, the unyielding one. The credit card with the painfully high interest rate that her husband had maxed out at the casino. She had nothing to show for this debt. No house, no car, no furniture, nothing of any value. He'd used it to gamble and who knew what else. She'd been making minimum payments on it from the beginning, but with the interest rate so high, she wasn't making a dent in the principal. All that hard-earned money went into thin air. She needed the payment from Carrie Custer's wedding to get this credit card paid for, but she wouldn't have it until after the final bill was submitted, after the wedding next month.

And now that she had to take it easy, how would she do her job? Some of it could be done on her computer, but the majority of it would be hands-on decorating, managing and planning. She couldn't rely on Liv to do it all and then take her share.

Tears pinched the backs of Piper's eyes.

"Piper." Max came around the counter and put his hands on her shoulders to look her in the eyes. "Talk to me."

His gaze was so full of love and concern, she crumbled. The tears started to fall and she found herself in his embrace, the truth tumbling out. "My doctor is concerned that my body might be getting ready for labor far too soon and she wants me off my feet until—"

"Piper!" Max pulled back, a frown on his face. "What are you doing in the kitchen?"

He didn't give her a chance to explain that the doctor said she could still do some things around the house, just nothing strenuous. Max led her into the sitting room and then moved the throw pillows to one side of the couch and nudged her to sit there. He grabbed a blanket off the back of a chair and put it over her lap and then reached behind her and flipped on a lamp.

He was close and he smelled like The One, by Dolce & Gabbana. Piper just watched him, the tears subsiding as a gentle smile tilted up her lips.

Maybe it was nice to have someone help her, after all.

Max's heart pounded with worry as he got down on one knee by Piper's side to tuck the blanket in around her.

Piper's cool hand rested on his cheek and she ran her thumb over the lines between his eyes. "You don't have to look so serious, Max."

He stopped fussing over her and grew very still under the weight of her hand.

"I'm going to be okay," she said quietly. "As long as I take it easy and don't overdo it, the doctor said the baby and I should be just fine." She lowered her hand and gave him a gentle smile. "I haven't seen you look this worried since your mom's cancer scare in tenth grade."

Max took her hand in his, thinking about nothing but Piper. "Tell me exactly what the doctor said."

"She said I need to stay off my feet as much as possible. No house work or exercising. I can still do a few things, but she doesn't want me on my feet for more than ten or fifteen minutes at a time." Piper looked down at the blanket on her lap and he could see that, even though she was trying to be brave for his sake, she was wrestling with her emotions. "We'll take it a week at a time. If she thinks things look better next week when I go in to see her, she'll lift the restrictions. But for now," Piper shrugged, "she wants me to rest."

"Then that's exactly what you're going to do." Max touched Piper's chin and lifted it until she was looking into his eyes. "I know you, Piper. You're going to push the limit on this thing because you can't sit still. But I don't want you doing anything—do you understand? As your boss—and as your friend," he said a little quieter, "I am telling you to listen to the doctor."

"But I have so many things I need to—"

"No." He shook his head. "I'll do them."

"You'll clean the toilets and scrub the bathtubs?"

"Yes," he said, completely serious. "And I'll even change the bedding and wash the laundry. I'll do whatever I need to do to make sure you take it easy."

"What about my work with Liv? I have a baby shower I'm hosting here on Sunday for the pastor's wife."

"Don't worry about it," he said. "I'll call Liv and do whatever you two tell me to do. You can sit right here and direct me."

She gave him a skeptical look and he put his hand on his heart. "I'm serious, Piper."

"What about your own work? You're gone every evening with the team. And the playoffs start this week. You won't have any extra time—"

"I'll hire someone to help Mrs. Anderson in the evenings."

"It'll cost more money."

"I don't care how much it costs."

She let out a sigh. "You can use my income to pay for—"

"No." He wouldn't hear of it. The last thing he would do is withhold Piper's wages, especially now. "Let me worry about the finances," he said to Piper. "You just focus on taking care of yourself and the baby."

Piper's bottom lip began to quiver and she bit it to stop. He hated when she cried. She hadn't done it often when they were younger, so he knew when she cried, it was serious.

"Don't cry, Piper." He got off his knee and sat on the edge of the couch beside her. He took both her hands in his, feeling helpless. "What can I do to help?"

"You've done so much, Max." She met his gaze again and her eyes were swimming in tears. One fell down her cheek. "It's just—" She stopped.

"What?"

"No one has ever told me they'll worry about the finances for me." She tried to laugh, but it didn't come out sounding comical.

Of course. She had provided for her and her dad in high school and was dealing with the fallout of Nick's poor financial choices now. Had Piper ever felt financially stable?

"I wish I could take care of all your financial troubles," he said. "Since I can't, at least let me worry about this one."

"Deal," she said, and this time she did laugh as she wiped away a tear. "Sorry for crying. I've been a lot more emotional since I got pregnant." She put her hand on her stomach. "It seems to go with all the other strange symptoms."

"Don't apologize."

Her eyes suddenly lit up.

"What?" he asked.

"The baby is moving." A shy smile tilted her lips. "Would you like to feel?"

He'd never felt a baby inside the womb before, and until this moment, had never really wondered what it would feel like. But he found himself nodding.

Piper gently took his hand in hers and laid it against her stomach, resting her hand over his.

The baby rolled under his palm. Max's heart rate sped up unexpectedly and emotion clogged his throat. He had never experienced something so simple—yet so profound. It felt like nothing he'd ever expected. Again, the baby pressed against his hand, this time it didn't roll away, but stayed there.

Piper giggled. "I think it likes you."

Max met her gaze, amazement and shock making him speechless. "Th-that's the baby?" he asked.

She nodded, her eyes glowing. "That's the baby."

The baby rolled again and Max's hand lifted from the force of it. "I can't imagine what that feels like from your perspective," he whispered.

"It's pretty amazing," she said.

Piper's hand was still over Max's and her gaze was on his face, watching him respond to her child's movement.

Not for the first time, he wondered what it would have been like if this child had been his, and not Nick's. He couldn't explain it, but he already loved this little person even though he didn't know him or her. Would he still be around when the baby was born? More now than ever, he wanted to be there. He wanted to meet this tiny person.

He would have probably sat there for the rest of the afternoon if the teakettle didn't start to whistle.

"Thanks," he said as he slowly pulled his hand away from her stomach.

"For what?" she asked.

"For sharing this with me." Emotion lowered the timbre of his voice. "For letting me experience a little bit of this blessing."

The whistle grew louder and Max left Piper's side to make her some hot chocolate.

It was getting harder and harder to pull himself away from her—and the baby.

Chapter Ten

"I'm serious, Piper," Max said from the formal dining room where he was setting down a plate of cucumber sandwiches. "If I see you get off that sofa again, I'm calling this whole thing off."

Piper reluctantly lowered herself back to the ornate sofa in the parlor and had the urge to stick her tongue out at Max like she would have done if they were nine again.

"Just because I took my eyes off you," he said as he rearranged the bowl of fruit on the elegant table, "doesn't mean I don't know what you're doing in there."

It wasn't often that Piper just sat in the parlor. Actually, it was the first time since the remodeling was done that she'd spent any amount of time in the fancy room. But now that she was relegated to the sofa while Max, Liv and Mrs. Anderson prepared for the baby shower, she realized she didn't like the arrangement of the furniture. So, whenever Max left the dining room to retrieve another dish Mrs. Anderson and Liv were preparing in the kitchen, Piper had used the opportunity to move a lamp here, a footstool there, or a small plant from one spot in the room to the other. It wasn't strenuous or taxing, by any means, but Max was having none of it.

"You're worse than a prison guard," she teased, though she wasn't completely joking. Never, in all her life, had she rested as much as she had in the past five days—and it was all because Max watched her every move. If he couldn't be there, he made Mrs. Anderson promise to keep an eye on her.

"I know you too well." He straightened and looked over the table with a critical eye.

Piper smiled to herself. She never thought she'd see Max Evans care so much about the presentation of a baby shower.

"If we don't remind you what the doctor said, you'll push yourself too hard." He came to stand in the large opening between the dining room and parlor. He wore one of Mrs. Anderson's frilly flower aprons over his button-down shirt and slacks. The older woman had insisted he put it on when he came back from church to help with the baby shower. She said his clothes were too nice to soil, and since he didn't want to argue with Mrs. Anderson, he gave in.

But now he stood there, his face stern, and Piper couldn't take him seriously. She bit the side of her mouth to keep from smiling at him.

"Don't try to soften me up, Piper Pierson Connelly," he said, wagging a finger as he started to smile. "I'm not wearing this apron for nothing. If I find out you're breaking the rules anyway, I'll make you walk around in a football uniform at the next baby shower you host."

"Oh, really?" She giggled. "I'd like to see you try."

"You two stop that," Mrs. Anderson said as she came

into the dining room with a large bowl of punch. "This baby shower is starting in a couple of minutes and we still need to set out the fresh flowers Liv just brought into the house." She set the punch down on the sideboard and then took Max by the arm. "Leave Piper be. She's a big girl. She doesn't need to be babysat every moment of the day."

"Doesn't she?" Max asked as he gave Piper a pointed look.

"Go on," she said with another laugh. "I promise I won't rearrange the whole room."

It was another dreary day outside, with rain falling and taking beautiful colored leaves off the trees. But in the house, the air was warm and redolent with the delicious aroma of fresh-baked scones, flowers and home-brewed coffee. The gray sky outside made the Tiffany stained glass at the top of the bay windows shimmer brightly.

Piper had gone to church that morning and then hurried home with Max to prepare for the shower. Mrs. Anderson had stayed behind to check out their weekend guests and to get all the last-minute food prepared for the late luncheon. But now, as everything was just about ready, Piper sat all on her own in the parlor waiting for the mom-to-be and her guests to arrive.

It felt strange to be doing nothing. Piper didn't like it one bit. She had started the event planning business because she loved hosting parties—not to sit around and watch everyone else do all the work.

The front doorbell rang and Piper rose to greet their guests. At least that was something she could do.

But Liv flew in from the private section of the house

and put her hand up to stop Piper from moving. "I've got it," she said. "Just stay there."

"I'm not going to sit here for Kate's party," Piper said. Yes, she was one of Kate's friends, but she was also the coordinator and hostess for the party. She couldn't just sit in the parlor the whole time like a bump on a log.

"Sit, Piper," Liv said as she disappeared into the foyer.

Frustration bubbled up in Piper's chest. Her friends were trying to take care of her, but it was starting to get annoying.

"Hello, hello," Liv said in the entry. "Welcome. Come on in. Piper's in the parlor. Go ahead and make yourselves comfortable."

Piper stood, unwilling to meet all the guests sitting down.

"Hello, dear." Max's mom was the first to enter. She set a wrapped gift on the table along the wall designated for the presents and then came over to Piper and gave her a hug. "How are you feeling?" she asked.

"I feel great." It was true, which made all of this so much harder to deal with. Her doctor told her that her body might be preparing for early labor, but Piper couldn't tell the difference.

"Max told me what's going on." She looked Piper over from head to foot. "But you look fabulous."

"Thank you."

Right behind Mrs. Evans, Joy Asher walked into the parlor with Kate Dawson, the lady for whom the shower was being thrown. The two women were visiting as if they hadn't just seen each other at church.

"Hello, Piper," Kate and Joy both said, waving at Piper.

Kate was beautiful in a long maxi dress, her blond hair loosely curled. She had been a Broadway actress before she had come to Timber Falls the year before to care for her cousin's triplets, but she had quickly fallen in love with their pastor who was a widower with a little girl. Piper had been in the throes of her own marital issues at the time and had not gotten to know Kate until after Nick's death when Kate and Pastor Jacob had spent so much time at the bed-and-breakfast helping.

Kate was radiant and her pregnancy was going well. A niggle of envy wedged into Piper's heart as she watched Kate laughing beside Joy, carefree and blissfully happy. Kate's husband would be at home, holding down the fort with their eight-year-old daughter and two-year-old triplets. When Kate went home tonight, her husband would be there waiting with open arms.

Piper pushed aside her self-pity and chose to smile for her friend, instead.

And that's when she noticed that both Joy *and* Kate were setting gifts down on the table. Why had Kate brought a gift to her own shower?

Dozens of other ladies walked into the parlor, all of them laden with gifts and smiles, and all of them hugging and greeting Piper. Very few of them made a special effort to greet Kate who stood to the side with Joy as they continued to visit.

Mrs. Anderson came into the room and was greeted by Mrs. Caruthers, Mrs. Topper and Mrs. Evans, the church ladies who had been so helpful after Nick's death.

But it wasn't just ladies from church who crowded

into the parlor and spilled over into the dining room. Neighbors started to enter, as well as a few friends from school that Piper had known almost all her life. Did they know Kate, too?

Liv was the last to enter the room, pushing her way through the swell of ladies to come and stand beside Piper.

"Well?" Liv asked. "What do you think?"

"What do you mean?" Piper asked.

Liv grinned and squeezed Piper's arm, then she called out to the room, "Ladies, if I could get your attention please." She waited until the room quieted and everyone turned to look at her and Piper. "I think it's time. At the count of three. One…two…three—"

"Surprise!" Everyone seemed to shout at once, laughter and conversation filling the room.

"It's *your* baby shower," Liv said to Piper, a giggle in her voice. "This one's for you, Piper."

Piper stared in shock as all the ladies smiled in her direction. The tableful of gifts was overflowing, there were more women inside the house than Piper could count from where she was standing and all of them had come just for her.

Max entered the dining room at that moment, still wearing Mrs. Anderson's ridiculous apron. He stood a head above all the ladies, so she was able to see his face clearly. He winked at her, his smile brighter than anyone else's.

She was speechless.

"Where will I put everything?" Piper asked as she looked around the parlor, her face glowing with awe.

"I—" She paused and shook her head. "I don't even know what to think right now."

Max sat on one of the wingback chairs in the parlor, exhausted and thankful the house was finally quiet again. Liv sat on the couch next to Piper, and Mrs. Anderson was in the other wingback chair. All the guests had left, and in their wake, it looked as if a baby store had exploded all over the parlor and dining room. Max had no idea a baby needed so much *stuff*.

But it was Piper, who sat in the middle of all the baby gear, who had his complete attention. He hadn't seen her look this happy in years. His chest was still bursting with the appreciation he'd felt for all the ladies who had come to shower Piper and the baby with their love and affection.

The longer he spent in Timber Falls, the more he realized how important it was to be a member of a supportive community.

"Thank you," Piper said as she looked from Mrs. Anderson to Liv, and then finally to Max, her heart in her eyes. "I'm so overwhelmed by your thoughtfulness."

"It was our pleasure," Liv said as she leaned over and gave Piper a side hug. "I'm not happy that you've been put on rest, but honestly, I didn't know how we were going to pull this off without you doing all the work for your own baby shower. I was trying to think of a dozen different reasons I could have sent you away from the house today while we prepared, but in the end, it all worked out."

"This whole time, this shower was meant for me and not Kate?" Piper asked. "Even when Joy called and scheduled the date with me—and told me the shower was for Kate?"

"Yes. It was actually Kate and Joy's idea," Mrs. Anderson said, her smile huge. "Wasn't it brilliant?"

Piper just shook her head, a smile lighting up her face as her gaze wandered over all the gifts. "I guess I'll have to store everything for now." Her voice came down a notch in disappointment. "The baby isn't due for two months and hopefully, by the time he or she comes, I'll have my own house to set it all up in."

"It definitely won't all fit in your little room," Mrs. Anderson agreed.

"What a shame," Piper said, almost to herself as she picked up the box with a baby monitor inside. "It would be fun to get it all organized."

"I remember having that feeling when my children were on their way," Mrs. Anderson said. "They call it 'nesting,' kind of like how a bird builds its nest for its babies. A mother also wants to prepare her little nest before her baby comes along."

Max's heart started to pound and he knew it was time to give Piper the gift he'd been preparing. Though he knew she'd love it, he also knew she might reject it, as well. He'd almost felt foolish when the idea first came to him, but the way it made his pulse race, he knew it was the right thing to give her. But over the past couple of weeks, as he'd put everything into place, he'd waffled between feeling excited and feeling depressed. Once he gave it to her, there was no going back.

"I wonder where I'll store it," Piper said. "Maybe the garage rafters?"

"I know where this stuff can go." Max stood, trying not to show his nerves. He extended his hand to Piper. "I'll show you."

Everyone stared at him in question as Piper frowned and took his offered hand.

"While you show Piper what you have in mind," Mrs. Anderson said, "Liv and I will start cleaning up this mess."

"Leave some for me," Max told her. "I'll come back to help after I show Piper the gift I have for her."

"Gift?" Piper stopped following him. "You didn't have to get me something, Max."

"I wanted to." It was all he would say. He didn't want her to reject his gift—especially here in front of the other two.

He went to the entry and started up the stairs. Piper followed him, curiosity and confusion marring her brow.

Max took a steadying breath as he walked down the upstairs hall to the steps that went up to the third-floor apartment.

"It's in your apartment?" Piper asked.

"Do you think you can manage the steps?"

She nodded. "I haven't been on my feet much at all today."

Max opened the door to the third-floor stairway and she went up in front of him. When they entered his apartment, the last of the day's sunlight filtered through the lead glass windows. Max flipped on a light and the main part of the apartment lit up. The space had previously belonged to Piper and Nick. It was still furnished, no doubt with their furniture.

Piper looked around the room for a heartbeat and Max wondered what memories came back to her while she stood there. Were they happy or sad? It had been six months since Nick died and almost two months since Max had come home. He didn't know how long Piper had been living downstairs. Did she miss the apartment?

"You're a lot tidier than you used to be," Piper teased.

"I knew you'd be coming up here today," he teased back.

She clasped her hands and looked at him expectantly, but didn't say anything.

This was the moment Max had been preparing for, but as he stood there with Piper, he was as nervous as the day he asked her to be his girlfriend. They'd only been in fifth grade at the time, but he remembered the moment like it was yesterday. Just like then, he didn't know where to start or exactly how to express himself.

"It's okay, Max," she said with a gentle smile, her dimple appearing in her cheek. "Just say it."

All his nerves disappeared. It was exactly what she had said to him in fifth grade, too.

"I'll just show you." He took her hand and led her to one of the bedroom doors. It was the room with the most daylight as it faced south under one of the large dormer windows. It was also the room closest to the master bedroom.

Max opened the door and stood there for a second as Piper stared at the room.

It was the most charming nursery Max had ever seen, and he'd done it all on his own—well, he'd had some help.

Piper's mouth slipped open and she blinked several times before she turned and looked at Max. "What is this?" she whispered.

"It's the baby's bedroom."

"Max." Her voice held a tone of incredulity.

"Mrs. Anderson told me you were registered at the baby store downtown, so I went there and asked them to put together everything you'd need for your nursery." He stepped into the room and drew her in with him. "I had no idea what I was doing, so the ladies at the store gave me the suggestion for the wall color and the curtains and the rug."

The room was painted a creamy color the ladies at the store had called ecru, and the curtains at the large window were a soft white. On the wood floor was a rug that matched the color of the curtains. The crib, changing table, dresser, shelf and armchair with ottoman were all a darker shade of a grayish brown. There were splashes of soft blue and pink in the bedding, a throw pillow, a teddy bear and a few other odds and ends.

"All it needs is a baby," Max said softly.

Piper let go of his hand and turned slowly, taking in every little detail.

But all Max could do was watch Piper.

When she finally turned all the way around, she looked at him again and tears were streaming down her face.

"Oh, Piper," he said as he went to her and pulled her into a hug, her tears tugging at his heart. "Why are you crying now?"

"Why did you do this?" she asked.

"I wanted to give you and the baby a present." He held her close. "But this isn't all."

"What?" she shook her head and pulled away.

"After the baby is born, and you can manage the stairs, I want you to move up here. You and the baby."

Her eyes filled with alarm and she started to shake her head.

"I'll move out first," he said quickly, suddenly realizing how his words might have sounded to her. "There's no reason you need to look for your own house when you already have a home here."

"But this isn't my home—"

"It is," he said with finality. "For as long as you want it to be."

"Where will you live?"

"The baby's not due until the end of December, right?" he asked.

She nodded.

"By then, my job at Timber Falls High will be done." He couldn't meet her gaze. "I'll probably be in California in December."

Piper put her hand on the crib and ran her slender fingers along the top rail. "Does that mean you'll take the job Margo's father offered?"

"I think so." He put his hands in his pockets and shrugged. "Unless something better comes along."

"It's a good opportunity, isn't it?" she asked.

He nodded. "It's a great opportunity. I'd be a fool to turn it down."

"Have you told her yet?"

"Who? Margo?"

Piper didn't answer, but nodded as she studied the crib.

"Margo has nothing to do with the job." He paused, because it wasn't completely true. If it wasn't for his relationship with Margo, Max probably wouldn't have gotten to know Tom Sutton so well, and he probably wouldn't have offered Max the job. "I'll be working with her father, Tom Sutton."

Piper turned her gaze back to Max to study his face. "Have you told Mr. Sutton you'll take the job?"

"Not yet. He said I had some time to make my decision." But now that he had, there was nothing to prevent him from calling Tom tonight.

"What will happen to the bed-and-breakfast?" she asked next, looking away from him again.

"I'll keep it until you're ready to buy it from me." He wanted her to look at him, needed to know what she was thinking. Was she angry at him for agreeing to take the job in California? Was she happy for him? Did she want him to go? "Or until you're ready to move on and do something else with your life."

"Can you afford to hold on to it that long?"

"Piper." He walked over to her and touched her chin so she'd look at him. "I told you not to worry about the finances."

She was quiet for a moment, and then she said, "Thank you." She straightened her back and laid her hand on her stomach. "I don't deserve any of—"

"You deserve every bit of it—and more." He wished he could give her so much more, but he respected her too much to press her for something she wasn't willing or able to give him.

"I don't think I should accept it," she said next. "It's too much."

"I didn't hear you tell anyone downstairs that you wouldn't accept their gifts, no matter how big or small." He stayed near the crib, though all he wanted to do was go to her and pull her into his arms again. "So I won't let you turn down my gift, either." He nodded toward the rest of the apartment. "There are three other bedrooms up here and I'm only using one. There's plenty of space for you to store all your other gifts and set up everything exactly how you want it."

She put one hand to her cheek. "Are you sure?"

"I'm positive. I'll haul it all up here myself."

"Max, I don't know how to thank you." Appreciation shined from her face. She didn't need words to tell him how much this meant. Her face said it all.

"You already have."

She came to him and wrapped her arms around him. Her stomach pressed against his and he couldn't help but think that he'd never felt anything as wonderful as her, and her child, in his arms.

Chapter Eleven

"I've decided a DJ is just too impersonal for my wedding," Carrie Custer said to Piper and Liv as they sat in the dining room of the bed-and-breakfast on the following Friday morning. "I think we should go with the original plan and hire a live band."

Piper pressed her lips together and took a deep breath through her nose, all the while trying desperately to stay patient. "Your wedding is two weeks from tomorrow, Carrie," she said slowly. "It would be impossible to find a decent band with such short notice."

"My father is paying you for the impossible, right?" Carrie asked. "This is my one and only wedding, shouldn't it be exactly what I want?"

Liv glanced at Piper and Piper knew exactly what she was thinking. By the time the wedding came, Carrie would probably change her mind about a dozen more details. The bride had no idea what she actually wanted and Liv and Piper had spent the past year trying to give her all the options, while steering her in a semirealistic direction.

"I'll see what I can do about a band," Liv said to Carrie. "Any particular band you have in mind?"

Carrie shrugged. "When I hear them, I'll know."

"Hear them?"

"Of course. I need to listen to them before I choose which one to hire."

"As in a live performance?" Piper asked.

"Preferably."

"There's not enough time to set up live auditions," Liv said. "I'll send you some links to the bands I contact." Liv didn't ask her if that would be okay. They were at the point where they simply had to tell the bride how it was going to be.

"Well," Carrie said on a sigh as she looked over the folder she had brought with her to today's meeting. "I suppose that's all I have for today. I'll call or text you if I have any other ideas."

Piper hoped and prayed she wouldn't have any other ideas. She had already changed the menu, the centerpieces and the DJ just today.

Liv and Piper stood, indicating the meeting was over.

"Thanks for all your help," Carrie said as she gathered her things together. "Can you believe the wedding's only two weeks away? The time has flown by."

Maybe for the bride-to-be, but for Piper, it felt like an eternity since the day Carrie had contacted them about the wedding.

"Ta, ta," Carrie said with a wiggle of her fingers. "I'll show myself out."

Piper and Liv sat back down at the table and waited until the door was closed behind Carrie before they both let out a sigh of relief.

"I cannot wait until this wedding is over," Liv said

as she lowered her forehead onto her forearms. "This woman is going to be the reason I never coordinate a wedding again."

Piper smiled and pulled together the notes she had taken while visiting with Carrie. "It's been a challenge," she conceded, "but it's almost over."

Liv pulled herself up and put her chin in her hand. "How are you feeling?"

"Great." Piper smiled. "I had my appointment with Dr. Meeker on Wednesday and she said everything looks stable. She told me she doesn't want me doing housework or exercising, but she lifted the other restrictions. She said I'm free to be on my feet and go about my normal routine, as long as I don't do anything strenuous. If something changes, I need to let her know immediately."

"And have you been listening to her advice?" Liv lifted her eyebrow, clearly skeptical of Piper.

"Max and Mrs. Anderson aren't giving me any choice." They'd been like mother hens to her all week. "Max even suggested that going up and down the stairs to his apartment more than once a day is too much for me."

"Have you been going up there often?" Liv pretended to be innocent, but Piper heard the hidden question.

"Yes, but only to arrange the baby's things." She had been up there every day since Sunday, folding and refolding the baby's clothes, organizing the drawers, setting up the nursery. Max had helped hang a couple of shelves and hauled up all the gifts. He helped her put together all sorts of things she would have struggled to figure out on her own. They'd assembled the swing, wrestled with the hamper, put together the diaper pail and rearranged some of the furniture to make it all fit.

"How are things going between you?" Liv asked gently. "From the outside, you two look as close as you used to be."

Piper shook her head. "To be that close, there would have to be a level of trust and intimacy that's no longer between us." How could there be when Piper still held him at arm's length when it came to her heart?

"Is that his choice or yours?"

Liv was one of Piper's dearest friends and they'd been through a lot together. Piper trusted her completely and knew that sharing her heart about Max would be safe—but she still hesitated because she wasn't even sure how she felt. She was afraid if she talked about it, she might come to some conclusions that terrified her—but maybe she was ready to face the truth.

Maybe.

"It's my choice," she said as she toyed with a piece of paper.

"Has he asked for more?"

"He asked if I might give him a second chance."

Liv sat up straight. "And you said no? Why?"

"Why?" Piper frowned. "You know why."

"Are you going to hold his sins against him forever?"

Liv's question felt like an arrow to Piper's heart. "I forgave him a long time ago—that doesn't mean I should open myself up to being hurt again."

"Do you think Max is the same man he was at the age of eighteen?"

"Of course not."

"Then what makes you think he'd hurt you again?"

Piper couldn't look Liv in the eyes. "I've been hurt

far too many times in the past to give him the opportunity."

"So you're holding your parents' faults and Nick's faults against Max?" Liv put her hands in her lap and shook her head. "That's a lot of guilt for Max to shoulder that he's not responsible for. Do you think that maybe you've saddled him with their mistakes because they're not here to blame?"

Was that what she was doing? Placing all her hurt and blame on Max because her parents and Nick weren't there to take it upon themselves? The very thought of it made Piper's stomach turn.

"Maybe you've forgiven Max," Liv said, "but until you forgive your parents and Nick, you'll never be able to move forward with anyone." Her voice was sad. "And you might miss the one opportunity in your life to love and be loved unconditionally by a man who has always meant the world to you. I know Max has his faults, we all do, but I've never met two people who were better friends or more suited to one another than you two. It would be the greatest travesty of your life to let that go a second time."

Tears gathered in Piper's eyes and she put her hand on her tummy. "What if he hurts me again?"

"He might," she admitted. "No one is perfect. But love is perfect, and when you love someone, you offer and receive forgiveness over and over and over again. You don't try to hurt the people you love, but it happens, and when it does, the Bible tells us that love is there to cover a multitude of sins."

Piper's heart rate started to speed up as Liv spoke truth to her. "I'm scared," Piper said quietly. "There's just too much at stake."

"Maybe." Liv shrugged. "But that's life in general. If we don't take the risks, we never succeed at anything. You took a risk starting a business, and buying this house and having a baby. But aren't those risks worth all the hard work and pain?"

Both of them were quiet for a moment, and then Liv asked Piper the one question that could answer all the others. "Do you love him?"

A tear slid down Piper's cheek and she nodded, unable to lie to her friend, or to herself, any longer. "I never stopped loving him. He's my best friend in the whole world and always has been, even when he was gone those ten years." Guilt washed over her and she quickly added, "I loved Nick, too, and when I married him, I truly believed my love for Max had died—but now I realize it only went dormant. Now that he's a part of my life again, it's suddenly reemerged, like a tender new plant, reaching toward the sun. I tried so hard to keep it from growing, but it's almost impossible."

"What will you do about it?"

Piper shrugged. "Nothing."

"Nothing?" Liv frowned. "Why?"

"Because he's taking a job in California and I have no wish to leave Timber Falls."

"Tell him how you feel."

"I can't." Piper shook her head. "I can't ask him to turn down such an amazing opportunity."

"Shouldn't that be his choice?"

"Maybe—but it's my choice, too, and I love him too much to let him toss everything away for me." She thought about their senior year in high school and the night before he went to Minneapolis for the championship game. She knew he had a good chance to play professional football, but the truth was, she had no desire to leave Timber Falls then, either. She couldn't explain it other than the fact that she'd moved a lot as a kid and Timber Falls had been the only place that felt like home.

Max had told her he'd give up his dream to play professional football for her, but she knew it would never work. He'd eventually resent her and she couldn't live with herself if he did. But if she gave up her dream to have a simple life and own a bed-and-breakfast in Timber Falls, and had to move to a big, impersonal city to follow him, she might grow to resent him, too.

Ultimately, Max had cheated on her the very next day and she'd broken up with him, but she always suspected that one of the reasons she hadn't given Max a second chance was because both of them wanted different things.

Not much had changed. She still wanted to stay and he needed to go and live his best life.

The sounds of the Lumberjacks celebrating in the locker room still rang in Max's ears as he left Timber Falls High and walked out to the parking lot. They had won their first playoff game and the last game they would play on their own field that season. In one week, they would head thirty miles south to St. Cloud State University where they would play in the Huskey Stadium. If they won that game, they would head to Minneapolis to play in the Vikings' stadium for their semifinal game. And, if they won that game, they'd return two weeks later to play the championship game. Only three games stood between Max and the state championship title he should have earned for Timber Falls ten years ago.

The early November air was cold as Max smiled at several people waiting for the team to come out and celebrate. But it was Piper, who waited with Liv, bundled in their winter coats, that made Max's night complete.

"Congratulations!" Piper said to him with a grin on her pretty face.

"Were you at the game?" he asked.

"Liv and I stayed huddled together on the bleachers, out of the wind." She held up a large thermos. "And we brought hot chocolate to help keep us warm."

"It was a great game," Liv said to Max, putting her hand up for a high five. "Tad did an amazing job out there tonight. You must be proud of him."

"I am. He has such a natural instinct on the field. Some things can't be taught."

"Reminds me of his big brother." Piper smiled. "Sometimes, when I'm watching him play, I have to remind myself he's not you."

"I just hope he goes farther than I did." Max didn't regret retiring from the NFL. If anything, he felt free for the first time in over a decade. But, just like everything else, if he could go back, he would make better choices. Maybe he wouldn't have been such a disappointment to himself or the NFL.

"He has the advantage of your advice and experience to help guide him," Piper said.

"Hopefully he takes it." Nothing had changed since homecoming, though now that Max knew why Tad resented him, it was a little easier to understand where his brother was coming from. He could only hope and pray that in time Tad would forgive him and they could heal their relationship.

"Well," Liv said, "as much as I like to stand around

and feel like a Popsicle, I think I'm going to head home." She shivered. "I'll talk to you two later."

"Bye, Liv," Piper called out to her.

"Bye," Max echoed.

"What about you?" Piper asked Max. "Are you heading home?"

Max took a deep breath, allowing the cold air to fill his lungs. "I'm too amped up to head home now. I kind of feel like celebrating."

"Yeah?"

"Remember what we used to do after a football game?" he asked.

"Go to Benny's Pizza House." Piper's grin was broad. "Have you been there since you came back?"

Max shook his head. "And now, it's all I can think about." Benny's had the best pizza in town and was one of the oldest restaurants in Timber Falls. It had been a favorite hangout place with two separate dining rooms. One for the quieter crowd and one for the teens and families with a game room close by. "How would you like to join me?" he asked Piper.

She nibbled her bottom lip as she gripped the thermos with her mitted hands. "I don't know. Mrs. Anderson was kind enough to let me leave with a full house, but I should probably get back to see if she needs anything."

It was a weak excuse and they both knew it. After being in business for two months, it was clear that there was little need for two people to be on call on a Friday night. The guests rarely needed anything, and if they did, one staff member was more than enough.

If Piper didn't want to join him, though, he wouldn't force her. Yet—he didn't know how much longer he would be in Timber Falls. If the Lumberjacks didn't win next week, he'd be here for only seven more days. After that, there would be no reason for him to stay. "I'm sure Mrs. Anderson can take care of our guests." He nudged her playfully. "Let's go. For old time's sake."

"Well," she sighed. "Now that I have pizza on my brain, I don't think this baby will let me sleep until I've satisfied the craving."

He smiled and took her free hand to walk her to his car. "I'll drop you back off here when we're done."

Benny's Pizza House was on the north end of town. The pizzeria had been owned for over forty years by the same family and when Max and Piper entered, they were given a hearty greeting by Benny and his wife.

"Max Evans!" Benny said, coming out of the kitchen to give Max a hug. He pointed to a wall dedicated to local athletes, and there was Max in the center of them all in his first professional football uniform. "I've been waiting for you to come home and sign my pictures. Would you?"

"Sure." Max smiled at Piper who was gracious and patient. No matter where they went, when people showed him attention, she just stood to the side and let him shine. She had done it since they were kids and it made him appreciate her all the more. In his mind, she was the shining star and he would never compare, no matter how much people singled him out.

Max took the permanent marker from Benny and signed his picture, then he and Piper took a seat at one of the small booths in the quieter part of the restaurant. He took his cell phone out of his back pocket and set it on the table.

The smell of pizza crust, marinara and spices filled the air and made Max's stomach growl.

"Wow," Max said as he looked around the dim interior. "This place brings back a thousand memories. Do you remember what it looked like before it was remodeled?"

Piper smiled and nodded as she, too, looked around the restaurant.

There were a few other tables full and several people looked their way, whispering excitedly back and forth.

"Do you ever get tired of all the attention?" Piper asked.

"I didn't really have to put up with much of it before I came back to Timber Falls." He didn't bother to look at the menu, since he already knew what he wanted. "For the most part, when I was in the NFL, people only recognized me when I was out at large events. On a day-to-day basis, I could go about my business with little bother." But here, in Timber Falls, where people had known him his whole life, he couldn't go anywhere without being recognized. The same was true with Piper, though. Everyone knew her, too, they just weren't as curious.

The doors opened and a loud crowd of teenagers came into the building. Tad was among several other football players, their girlfriends and other friends. One of them noticed Max and they all turned to wave—all except Tad who led Shelby into the game room on the other side of the restaurant.

Piper watched Max closely. "Anything better with Tad?"

Max sighed and shook his head. "He still thinks I'm a phony. Doesn't want to take any advice or correction from me. Not only is he mad because I abandoned him and Mom, but he thinks I'm pretty much a loser who has nothing to contribute to his life." Max shrugged, trying to act like it didn't bother him, but then he remembered he was with Piper and she'd see right through his bluffing. "He thinks he'll do a better job with the talent he's been given, and maybe he will."

"He'll eventually mature and realize that life is hard and there were pressures you had to deal with that he didn't understand as a kid." Her cheeks were rosy from the cold and her eyes were still glowing from the excitement of the evening. There were a couple small creases at the corners of her eyes that hadn't been there in high school, but she had only grown more beautiful over the years.

"I hope you're right."

Rita approached. She'd been waitressing at the pizza house for decades and used to wait on them when they were in high school. Her skin was wrinkled and her hands were gnarled and worn from years of carrying trays, wiping tables and filling orders. She must not have heard the commotion when Max entered, because her eyes opened wide. "Max!" She looked at Piper, just as excited to see her. "And Piper! Look at you two. Just like old times." Her gaze slipped to Piper's midsection and she noticed the pregnancy. "And a baby, too? What a surprise. It's been so long since I've seen the two of you. How are you?"

"Good," Piper said. "And how are you?"

"Same old, same old." Rita grinned as she looked from Piper to Max, and then back to Piper. "You two are as cute as ever. I always thought there was something special between you. You're one in a million, you know that, don't you? Not everyone gets a love story like the one you two have."

Max looked at Piper, waiting for her to correct the waitress, but she didn't.

She just met Max's gaze, a gentleness in her eyes that made Max's heart race.

He wouldn't correct the waitress, either.

"What can I get for you?" Rita asked, apparently oblivious to the silent communication that had just passed between Max and Piper. "The usual?"

"Do you remember what we used to order?" Max asked, his incredulous gaze tearing away from Piper to look at Rita.

"Sure do. A large pepperoni pizza, order of garlic cheese bread and a pitcher of ice-cold root beer with two frosted mugs."

"Sounds perfect," Piper said as she handed her menu over to Rita. "Thank you."

"I'll throw in an extra slice of bread for that baby," Rita said with a wink. "Be back in a minute."

As she walked away, Max let his gaze settle on Piper again.

"What?" Piper asked.

"You didn't correct her when she thought we were still a couple."

Piper fiddled with the Parmesan shaker and shrugged. "It seemed the easiest way to handle the situation. Why go to the trouble of trying to explain the past ten years?"

"I'm surprised she doesn't know about what happened—and then Nick…" He let his sentence trail off.

Piper shrugged again. "Timber Falls is just big enough that we don't know everything about everyone. Unless she had a kid in school with us, or went to church with us or knew our parents, I'm not surprised she doesn't know all the details."

Max nodded, but he was still surprised Piper didn't correct her.

A silent pause filled the space between them, but Max wasn't afraid of silence with Piper. It was one of those things that told him a lot about a relationship. They were just as comfortable with the noise as they were the silence.

"Do you have everything you need for the baby?" he asked her.

"I think I'm all set." She smiled, but he could see the trepidation hidden in her eyes. "Less than six weeks to go."

"Are you scared?"

She pushed aside the Parmesan and clasped her hands. "I'd be lying if I said I wasn't."

He nodded. It would be hard enough to have a child—harder still to do it on her own. He longed to tell her he'd be there for her, if she wanted him, but he didn't want to press her. She knew it, even if he didn't tell her.

Max's phone rang and Margo's name showed up on his screen.

Piper glanced at the phone as Max switched off the ringer and turned the phone over. It still vibrated on the tabletop.

"Aren't you going to answer her?" Piper asked.

"No." Max had not returned any of her other calls or texts. She had tried contacting him half a dozen times, never telling him what she wanted, just telling him to call her.

"Have you told her dad you're going to take the job?"

"I haven't gotten around to it." He'd been busy with the team getting ready for their first playoff game—and a part of him had hoped Piper would tell him not to leave.

Her gaze was steady as she looked at him. "Don't put him off and miss your opportunity. You'd be good as a college scout, Max. I watch you with your team. You were born for the game of football—whether you're playing, coaching or scouting. How many job opportunities are there for you to use your talents and gifts that way? Don't let it slip away."

He watched her, trying to see how she really felt about him leaving. "Do you think I should take the job?"

"Yes." It was a simple, straightforward answer, with no reservations or regrets.

Piper wanted him to take the job in California, and the realization of it felt like a splash of cold water.

She didn't want him to stay.

Chapter Twelve

The high school commons buzzed with excitement as the team sat at the round tables, their parents and siblings sitting with them. They had won their second playoff game at St. Cloud State University and in the morning, they would head to the Vikings' stadium in Minneapolis to play their semifinal game. But, for tonight, they would celebrate their seniors, eat a meal together and build up morale for tomorrow's big game.

Max sat at a table with Tad and his mom, enjoying the chicken Kiev and wild rice pilaf. Piper and Liv had been hired to coordinate the banquet and they were darting in and out of the school kitchen where the caterer had set up.

They had done an amazing job personalizing the event, making unique centerpieces, filling the room with purple and black balloons for the school colors, and they'd even set up easels with boards honoring each senior. The seniors' pictures, football stats and other fun information was displayed.

"Piper should get off her feet," Mom said to Max as

she tugged on his sleeve. "Have her come and join us. She looks a bit pale."

It had been a week since they'd gone out for pizza, and in that week, he'd rarely laid eyes on her. She had spent almost every waking minute working on the Custer wedding—which was tomorrow—planning the football banquet and managing the bed-and-breakfast. He checked in with Mrs. Anderson every day to make sure Piper wasn't doing any of the physical work, and the older lady had assured him Piper was heeding the doctor's advice. But she was still too busy for his liking.

Max put his napkin down and walked over to where Piper was standing with Liv.

Piper's violet-blue eyes lit up when she saw him and his heart did a little flip at the sight. Would he never lose that funny little flutter he felt when seeing her?

"Are you two going to get a chance to eat tonight?" he asked.

Piper put her hand on her stomach and shook her head. "I don't have much of an appetite today."

"And I have to run," Liv said, her usually polished appearance a bit frazzled. "With the Custer wedding tomorrow, we're also overseeing the groom's dinner tonight. I'm heading there now and then going to the ballroom to make sure all the decorating is underway."

"Thanks a million," Piper said to Liv. "I'll be there in the morning to meet with the florist."

Liv gave Piper a quick hug. "See you tomorrow."

"Thanks for all your help with the banquet," Max said to Liv. "It turned out great."

Liv smiled and waved as she left the commons, her heels clicking on the hard tile floor.

"Would you like to join us?" Max asked Piper. "We've got more than enough room at our table."

Piper waved at Max's mom, who tried to motion her to come over. "I wish I could," Piper said, "but the caterer is wrapping things up in the kitchen and I need to get home to work on the seating arrangement for the wedding tomorrow. Carrie sent over a ton of last-minute changes to the chart. Apparently, some family members are fighting and she doesn't want them sitting near each other."

She glanced around the commons, exhaustion lining her face. "It looks like everything is all set here. Is there anything else you need from me?"

"I need for you to rest." He had his back to the loud group of football players and their parents and was speaking for her ears alone. "I'm worried about you."

She bit her bottom lip and didn't meet his gaze. "I appreciate the concern, but I don't have the luxury of a break right now. I need this wedding to go off without a hitch tomorrow. After that, I'll have all the time in the world to rest and relax."

He wished he could ease her burdens. He'd hired a part-time maid who came in on Mondays and Thursdays to clean the bed-and-breakfast and prep for the new guests. But he couldn't step in and hire someone to help Piper and Liv with their event business. And he knew Piper needed the wedding to be perfect, because she needed the money to pay off some debt. She didn't talk about it, and she was too proud to ask him for financial help, but he had ears and he'd heard enough over the past couple of months.

Even if he wanted her to take it easy, she couldn't.

"I wish I could come to the game in Minneapolis tomorrow," Piper said. "Hopefully you'll win and I can come to the championship game in a couple weeks."

"I'll plan on it."

She left and Max went back to his mom and brother. Excitement had ramped up and the team was louder than ever. After the meal was finished, it took several attempts, but Max was able to get the group's attention and had the honor of giving out awards, letting the seniors speak and then leading them in a pep talk.

By the time the evening wrapped up, Max was exhausted and ready to get some sleep before tomorrow's big game.

"There's a ton of food leftover," Max said to his mom when they were the last ones at the high school. There was a box of food he'd just taken out of the refrigerator and a stack of other odds and ends he needed to bring back to Piper. "Do you want to take some of it home?"

"What would I do with it?" she shook her head. "Why don't you take it back to the bed-and-breakfast and let Piper decide. Tad will help you."

Tad stood to the side with his cell phone in his hand. "What?" he asked.

"Help your brother with the food and the easels and things. He needs to get it all back to Piper."

Max didn't really need the help, but he wanted a chance to talk to Tad before tomorrow. "Come on," he said as he nodded toward the parking lot. "Give me a hand. I'll take you home later."

Tad rolled his eyes, but he grabbed the easels and the leftover centerpieces that people had forgotten on the tables.

"See you later," Mom said as she kissed first Max

and then Tad on the cheeks. "I'm heading home to bed. Big day tomorrow!"

"Bye, Mom," Max called.

Tad helped Max put everything in his car and then they left the parking lot.

It was only a few blocks to the bed-and-breakfast, but Tad didn't say a word. He still had his cell phone in hand. The glow from the screen illuminated the inside of Max's car.

"Who you talking to?"

"Shelby."

"Are you two pretty serious?"

Tad shrugged. "We've been dating for almost a year."

"Do you think you'll stay together once you go to college?"

Again, Tad shrugged. "Who knows?"

"Do you *want* to stay together?"

"I don't know." Tad's voice rose in irritation. "Why do you care?"

They pulled up to the bed-and-breakfast. The house was lit up with all the guests who had come in for the weekend. Piper had mentioned that everyone who was staying with them were guests for the Custer wedding. Max didn't want to disturb anyone with his and Tad's conversation, so he planned to talk to him in the car, but Tad got out and went to the back seat to start unloading everything.

"I care," Max said, getting out of the car, irritated that his brother was choosing to make things difficult. "Because I care about you and your future."

"You care if Shelby and I stay together or break up?" Tad shook his head. "Why?"

Max put his hands on the top of his car and looked

at his brother. It was dark, but there was enough light from the house to let him see Tad's face. "You're angry, because you feel like I abandoned you and Mom, but now you're angry because I'm back and I want to be a part of your life. Make up your mind, Tad. Either you want me to be a part of your life or you don't."

Tad slammed Max's door. "I don't need this from you."

He started walking toward the back of the bed-and-breakfast. Max followed him. "I want to talk to you and I want you to listen to me like a grown-up."

Tad opened the back door. The entry was dark, so Max reached around his brother and flipped on the light. Tad set down the easels and tried to move past Max to return to the car, but Max wouldn't let his brother leave the back entry.

"I'm going to give it to you straight, Tad, because I respect you and it's time for me to talk to you like an adult." Max was tired of tiptoeing around his brother. "I know you don't think highly of me and I'm okay with that. I messed up. But I don't want you to follow in my footsteps. There will be college scouts at the game tomorrow and they'll be there to watch you. You have the chance to play for some pretty prestigious colleges and you have a really great chance at going pro." Max put his hands on Tad's shoulders and forced him to look him in the eyes. "Don't make the same mistakes I made. Don't let this all go to your head. Be a man of integrity and don't trample anyone on your way to success."

Tad watched Max quietly, but he could see that he was finally getting through to his brother.

"I'm sorry you were one of the people I trampled," Max said, a little quieter, swallowing back the emotions clogging his throat. "I love you, Tad. If I could go back, I'd do things different. But I can't. All I can do is say I'm sorry and hope we can move forward."

Without warning, Tad embraced Max, just like he used to do when he was a kid. "I love you, too, Max. Why'd it take you so long to tell me?"

Max held his brother close. He thought he'd told his brother he loved him—but maybe he'd just assumed his brother knew.

"I'm scared, Max," Tad said. "What if I mess everything up?"

"Seek God first, and then find wise counsel. You'll be okay." He pulled back and looked at his brother. "And if you love Shelby, don't mess it up. I would give everything for a chance to go back and save my relationship with Piper. She means more to me than anything in the world, but I was a fool and I let her go. If Shelby is that important to you, don't let her go, Tad. Because at the end of your career, no matter how long that may be, you'll only have one thing left: your relationships. That's what you need to be guarding with all your heart. The rest will fall into place."

Tad stared at him. "Would you really give it all up for Piper?"

"In a heartbeat."

"The NFL?"

"Without a doubt in my mind." Max didn't even have to think about it. "Piper is more precious to me than football, money, fame or anything else this world has to offer." He smiled at his brother. "But, if you can have it all, go for it. You'll have the time of your life."

Tad let out a big sigh. "I'm sorry I've been such a jerk, Max."

"Don't worry about it." Max put his arm around his brother and knuckled him in the gut like he used to when they were younger. "I'm sorry it took so long for me to tell you I love you."

Tad laughed and tried getting Max back, but Max was still stronger than his kid brother.

"Come on," Max said. "Let's get the rest of this inside and then you need to get home and go to bed. You've got a lot riding on this game tomorrow."

"I'm happy you'll be there, Max."

"So am I. I wouldn't miss it for anything."

They brought the rest into the house and then Max drove his brother home. It felt good to have his little brother back.

Piper sat on her bed, her swollen feet stretched out before her, looking at the finished seating chart lying against the wall. Her back ached, her feet were sore and her head pounded.

But it was her heart that was in the most pain. The house was old and she had heard most of Max and Tad's conversation in the back entry. She hadn't meant to eavesdrop, but it had been impossible not to hear their heated words.

She laid her hands on her tummy, feeling the baby move beneath her palms, trying to ignore what she'd heard.

Max said he'd give it all up in a heartbeat for her. She had no reason to believe he'd lied to Tad—on the contrary, without knowing she could hear him, she suspected that he was being completely honest with his brother.

But it only confirmed what she already knew. Max

would have given everything up for her in high school—and he'd give it all up for her now, if she let him. She tried telling him not to pass up the opportunity to work for the University of California at Mid-State, and she hoped he was taking her seriously.

She suspected he was, or Margo Sutton wouldn't be calling him. Twice now she had seen her name on Max's phone and she wondered how often Margo called when Piper wasn't nearby. Was Max talking to her? He denied it the first time, but the second time, she didn't even ask him. Would they rekindle their romance once Max was working for her father? Margo would have so many connections for Max. He could go so far. Maybe he wouldn't play for the NFL again, but could he end up coaching a professional team some day? It was only a matter of time for someone to see what an incredible coach he was. She had witnessed it on the Lumberjacks' field and knew he could take his abilities all the way. Working as a college scout was simply the first step.

And no matter how much Piper loved him, and no matter how much she wanted to make a life with him, she wouldn't ask him to stay.

The baby rolled under her touch and she tried to smile, though her heart was heavy and she felt like crying. "It looks like it's going to be just you and me," she whispered to her child. "I'm so sorry."

The tears did come as she pulled the covers up to her chin and tried to find a comfortable position to let her weary body rest.

As hard as it was, she would keep her feelings to herself and encourage Max to leave Timber Falls—again.

Chapter Thirteen

The smell of bacon, fresh-baked muffins and coffee met Max on the back stairs as he came down from his apartment on Saturday morning. The sun was shining, the temperatures were higher than normal for mid-November and Max couldn't stop himself from whistling.

He set his duffel bag down in the back entry, smiling at the reminder of his conversation with Tad, and took his Lumberjacks jacket off the back hook. He had to meet the team bus in the parking lot in less than fifteen minutes for their two-hour drive to Minneapolis, but it would take only a couple minutes to drive to the high school. He had enough time to pop into the kitchen, grab something to eat, fill up a mug with some of Mrs. Anderson's coffee and get a glimpse of Piper—which was the real reason he opened the door into the private living space at the back of the main floor.

When he had come home from dropping Tad off last night, he had hoped she'd still be awake so he could talk to her. But she had already been in bed and the last thing he wanted to do was wake her up. What he had to say could wait for morning, but now that morning had come, he couldn't wait another minute.

"Good morning," he said when he saw Mrs. Anderson lifting a tray of steaming muffins off the counter.

"Morning, Max." She walked to the swinging door leading into the dining room and started to back through it. "Grab something to eat." She disappeared into the dining room, clearly busy.

Max glanced around the space, but didn't see Piper. Disappointment flogged him as he walked to the counter. He wanted to say goodbye to her before he left. They both had a big day, and though there was little he could do to help her with the Custer wedding, he still wanted to make sure she knew he'd be thinking about her.

He also wanted to ask her if she'd go out with him to celebrate tomorrow, because one way or the other, they'd both have a lot to be thankful for. But more than that, he wanted to tell her what he should have told her a long time ago.

He loved her—and it wasn't until he'd talked to Tad that he realized he needed to tell her. He couldn't just assume she knew. Even if she still sent him away, at least then he could go knowing he'd done everything he could.

A movement in the alcove under the stairs caught his eye and he turned to find Piper sitting at her desk.

"Hey," he said, his heart warming at the sight of her.

"Morning," she said with a sad smile on her lips. She looked amazing in a pair of tight black pants and a stylish steel-gray long-sleeved shirt that was fancy, yet functional. Her hair was styled up in an elegant twist and she wore a pair of black flats. Her pregnancy made her look prettier than ever, but it was his love for her that made her the most beautiful woman he'd ever laid eyes on.

She took his breath away.

But the sadness in her eyes and the way she winced when she stood made his smile fall. "What's wrong, Piper?"

"I'm just sore and tired."

He wanted to pull her into his arms and spend the day pampering her, but it would have to wait.

Telling her how he felt didn't have to wait—but did he want to tell her here, in the middle of the kitchen, with the chance that Mrs. Anderson might walk in at any minute? No. Piper deserved so much more than a rushed declaration in a busy house.

"I have to meet the bus soon," Max said, "but I was wondering if you and I can go somewhere tomorrow evening. Just the two of us. I'd like to celebrate—no matter what happens today—and—" he took a deep breath "—I'd like to talk to you about a few things."

Piper worried her bottom lip between her teeth as she studied him, hope and uncertainty waging a war in her gaze. "Where would you like to go?"

A smile tugged up the corners of his mouth. "I thought maybe we could eat at Ruby's Bistro and then take a walk in the park along the river." It had been one of their favorite dates in high school. They'd felt so grown-up making reservations at Ruby's and then taking their time strolling along the lamp-lit path in the park, hand in hand. Piper had often said the park was her favorite place in Timber Falls and there was a bench near the waterfalls that gave the town its name that she had claimed as their bench.

"It might be cold," she said.

"I'll bring a blanket to keep us warm and a large thermos full of hot chocolate."

She didn't answer him for what seemed like an eternity, but finally she nodded. "I'd like that, Max."

He couldn't hide his grin and was already imagining cuddling up under that blanket with her, admiring the stars, as he told her what was in his heart.

"I'm sorry I have to run," he said. "The bus will leave the parking lot whether I'm on it or not." He grabbed a travel mug and poured some coffee into it.

"Here," she said as she went to the counter and took a hot muffin off the cooling rack. "Don't forget to grab something to eat."

"Thanks." He took it from her and had to resist the urge to pull her into his arms and kiss her, right then and there.

"I'll walk you out," she said, surprising him.

He led the way to the back entry and she opened the door for him, since his hands were full. She also picked up his duffel bag. "What do you have in here?" she asked as she hefted the strap over her shoulder.

"Let me take that," he said.

"I've got it." She laughed as she opened the outside door and they walked toward his car.

His keys were in his jacket pocket, so he set his mug on the roof of his car to grab them.

"Nervous for today?" she asked him.

He shook his head. "Just excited. I wish my dad could be here to see Tad. My mom's driving down separately."

A black Porsche pulled up to the bed-and-breakfast and came to a stop near the parking area.

Max and Piper both turned to look—and Max's heart fell.

Margo.

She stepped out of the Porsche in a pair of black heels, her slender body clothed in tight jeans rolled at the ankles, and a long sleek jacket. She wore her blond hair in a high pony and had on a pair of dark black sunglasses. She'd come by her title as Miss California effortlessly as she carried herself like she was always on display. It was one of the reasons Max was happy to end it with her. He had never felt like he knew the real Margo Sutton. What he saw was what she wanted him to see—perfection. It was impossible to live up to and even more impossible to emulate.

And she liked it that way.

"Max!" Her smile was as dazzling as it had been when she competed in her pageants.

Piper watched Margo, almost as if she was in a trance, her mouth slightly ajar.

Margo pulled her sunglasses off as she walked right up to Max, her stride making her look like she was on a runway, and gave him a kiss on the lips. "Hello, handsome."

"Margo." He shook his head, horrified that she'd come all the way from California without giving him a warning—and more horrified that she'd take the liberty to kiss him in front of Piper. "What are you doing here?"

"What kind of a greeting is that?" Margo asked in a wounded tone. "I've missed you."

She glanced over at Piper, her large, sky blue eyes

slowly traveling over Piper from her toes up to her face. "Aren't you going to introduce me to your friend?" she asked Max.

Max shook his head, as if trying to clear out all the confusion. "Margo, this is Piper Pierson—Connelly," he added, almost as an afterthought. "She—" he paused. How did he explain who Piper was? His friend, his ex-girlfriend, his business partner, his employee? The woman he'd loved for most of his life? "She and I have been friends since we were kids."

Margo lifted a perfectly arched eyebrow. "How do you do?" Margo asked.

"And, Piper, this is Margo Sutton."

"Max's girlfriend," Margo said, offering Piper her hand.

Piper didn't take Margo's hand, but looked at Max, her eyes filled with questions and hurt.

Max shook his head to deny Margo's claims. "We broke up before I came," he said to Piper.

"We took a 'break,'" Margo corrected, using her fingers to make air quotes as she rolled her eyes playfully and wrapped her arm around Max's. "But I decided I wasn't going to let our break get in the way of coming to Minnesota to support you. Daddy told me your team was going to the playoffs, so I thought I should come and cheer you on."

"How did he know?" Max hadn't taken the time to call Mr. Sutton yet, holding out hope that he'd have a reason to stay in Timber Falls.

"He knows everything, Maxwell." Margo smiled at Piper, who was still holding Max's heavy duffel bag— not saying a word.

Max slid his arm loose from Margo and took the bag from Piper.

His phone rang and he knew it would be his assistant coach, wondering where he was. The bus would need to leave if the team wanted to get to the stadium on time.

"I need to go," he said, wishing he could stay and explain things to Piper. "The team is waiting for me."

"I can drive you wherever you need to go," Margo said.

"We're heading to Minneapolis." Max opened his car door to shove his duffel bag inside.

"I just came from the Minneapolis airport," Margo said on an impatient huff. "But I can drive you back."

"I need to be with my team."

"What am I supposed to do?" Margo asked.

Max shrugged, his stress level rising with each beat of his heart. Piper looked so hurt and confused. She started to take a step backward toward the house. He couldn't let her go without convincing her Margo wasn't his girlfriend.

"Let me drive you," Margo said, sidling up to Max as if Piper wasn't standing there. "I'll drop you off at the stadium and that'll give us time to talk."

"I can't, Margo."

"Max." She put her hands on her hips. "I came all this way and you're going to abandon me? I just want to talk and tell you what Daddy has said about the job. It's really exciting. He has big plans for you."

Max's phone continued to ring, so he pulled it out of his pocket and answered. It was Greg, his assistant coach.

"Where are you, Max? We need to get going."

"I'm sorry, Greg. Something came up. Do you mind meeting me at the stadium?"

Greg was silent for a second, but then he said, "Sure. I'll plan to see you there."

"Thanks." It wasn't how Max envisioned his day starting, but the sooner he could talk to Margo, the sooner he could send her back to California.

Margo grinned at him. "Let's take the rental." She motioned toward the Porsche. "Isn't that better than riding on the stinky bus?" She started walking back to her car.

Max grabbed his duffel bag, shut the car door and took the mug of coffee off the top of his Lexus. He still held the muffin, but it was now crumbled in his clenched hand.

"Piper." He shook his head, wishing he had time to explain. "It's not what you think, please believe me. I'll explain it all when I come home."

"You don't have anything to explain, Max." She lifted her shoulders, pain in her gaze. "I hope everything goes well for you today."

She turned and headed back toward the bed-and-breakfast.

"Piper!" he called to her, but he didn't have time to chase her.

Piper walked into the bed-and-breakfast, unable to catch her breath. The Porsche pulled away from the house with a squeal and Piper couldn't help but wonder what Max wasn't telling her. A woman didn't just fly across the country on a whim to "support" an ex-boyfriend unless there was something else going on between them. Were they still a couple? Had Max been lying to her?

Anger and hurt mingled in her chest and she pressed herself against the closed door. Max had looked cornered—trapped—caught. And now he was in a vehicle with Margo Sutton, heading to Minneapolis. What would they talk about? What plans did her father have?

Piper forced herself to calm down. This was what she wanted, wasn't it? An opportunity for Max to succeed.

But why did Margo have to look so amazing and svelte when Piper felt like an overinflated balloon?

"What's wrong, Piper?" Mrs. Anderson asked when she walked into the room. She set down an empty juice carafe and rushed over to Piper. "Is it the baby?"

"No." Piper shook her head. She was being silly—she was just shocked, that was all. Max didn't owe her any explanation.

So then why did it hurt so much to see him with Margo?

"I need to get to the ballroom," Piper said, straightening to her full height and running her hands over her hair. "The florist should be there with the flowers and I need to make sure they're set out according to plan."

"Take a minute to sit down and tell me what's going on," Mrs. Anderson said. "You're as white as a bedsheet."

Piper put her hand up to her face. Her fingers were trembling and her brow felt warm.

"Maybe I will sit down." As she moved from the door to the chair, the first contraction squeezed across her abdomen and took her breath away.

"What's wrong?" Mrs. Anderson asked.

The pain was so intense, Piper couldn't speak. She bent forward and gasped.

"I'm taking you to the hospital," Mrs. Anderson said.

"But it's too early," Piper said between clenched teeth. The pain soon subsided, but she was still weak and shaky.

"I don't care. Something's not right, Piper."

"You can't leave. We have guests."

"I don't care."

"And I need to get to the ballroom."

"It will all have to wait."

Piper wouldn't risk her baby's life for anything, so she nodded. "But let me call Mrs. Evans," Piper said. "She can be here in five minutes and take me to the hospital. We can't both leave the house with all these guests."

Mrs. Anderson squinted her eyes in thought, and then nodded. "Fine. I'll call her."

As she pulled out her cell phone, another contraction came on and Piper pressed her eyes closed, trying not to whimper. "Please," she prayed silently to God. "Please keep my baby safe."

Less than five minutes later, Mrs. Evans arrived in a whirlwind of concern. With barely a word, she whisked Piper away from the house. Thankfully, Mrs. Anderson had been able to throw a few essential items into a bag for Piper, in case the baby wanted to be born early.

All the way to the hospital, Mrs. Evans peppered her with questions, asking how far apart the contractions were, what she'd had to eat that morning and so on. "I'll call Max as soon as we get you checked into the hospital," she said. "He'll want to know what's happening."

At the mention of Max, Piper started to cry. She

wanted him by her side more than anything, but he was currently on his way to Minneapolis with another woman.

When they reached the hospital, Piper was immediately brought back to the ER where a flurry of nurses took her vital signs, asked dozens of questions and set her up on a fetal monitor. Dr. Meeker was paged at the clinic and Piper was left with Mrs. Evans to wait.

"I can't get ahold of Max," Mrs. Evans said as she walked into the room where Piper was lying. It was a stark environment, with fluorescent lights and a strange, chemical smell. Her blood pressure was high, but the nurse said that was to be expected with all the commotion. It wasn't high enough to worry them—yet.

"I called Tad, but he said Max isn't on the bus with them." Mrs. Evan's eyes—so much like Max's—were filled with worry.

"He's driving to Minneapolis with Margo Sutton."

Mrs. Evans's mouth thinned into a straight line. "Margo's back in his life?"

"She showed up unexpectedly, so he got into her car."

Mrs. Evans took a deep breath before she said, "He must have turned off his ringer, because he's not answering."

Another contraction wrapped around Piper's middle and she had to close her eyes to block out the harsh lights.

Mrs. Evans was at her side, rubbing her arm and speaking calm words to her. Piper thanked God Max's mom was there. When it had really mattered, Mrs. Evans had always been a second mother to her, just like now.

"Thank you," she whispered to Mrs. Evans when the contraction passed. "I know you planned to be on your way to Minneapolis right now—"

Dr. Meeker came around the corner, her white coat flapping as she rushed to Piper's side, her face drawn. "It looks like you'll be getting that trip to Minneapolis, after all," she said to Piper and Mrs. Evans. "I don't like what I'm seeing on the fetal monitor, Piper." Her voice was calm, but serious. "You're only thirty-five and a half weeks along. We consider a baby preterm if they come before thirty-seven weeks, which puts you and the baby at high risk. Your body is in labor, and given all the information my associate was able to attain, I don't think we can stop it. We don't have a neonatal intensive care unit here in Timber Falls, so I'm having you airlifted to Abbott Northwestern Hospital in Minneapolis. You can deliver there and the baby will be taken care of by world-class physicians." She studied Piper. "Are you okay with that plan?"

Tears gathered in Piper's eyes, but she nodded. "Whatever I need to do for the baby."

Dr. Meeker nodded and patted Piper's shoulder. "I've already ordered the medicopter. It should be here within a half an hour." She glanced at Mrs. Evans and then back to Piper. "You may take one guest with you—" She was stopped by a nurse needing more information for the air ambulance team. "I'll be back in a few minutes to give you more information," Dr. Meeker said. "Try not to worry, Piper. We'll make sure you and the baby have everything you need to be safe and healthy."

Piper nodded as she watched her doctor slip out of the room. Her gaze then landed on Mrs. Evans and tears streaked down Piper's face. "I'm so sorry," Piper said. "I know you wanted to be with Tad and Max today."

"Hush," Mrs. Evans said, coming to Piper's side. "Don't even give it another thought, Piper. I'm here for you. Nothing is more important than you and the baby right now."

"Thank you." She closed her eyes to try to focus. Everything was happening so quickly. It wasn't supposed to be this way. She had a wedding to coordinate today—she needed the money desperately, but what choice did she have? "I need to call Liv and tell her what's happening, she'll need to oversee the Custer wedding—"

"I'll call her."

"And Mrs. Anderson needs to know what's happening—"

"I'll call her, too. And, if it's okay with you, I'm going to get the prayer chain started for you at church." She waited for Piper to nod, and then she said, "You just rest, Piper." She ran her hand over Piper's forehead and moved aside some hair that had fallen out of place. "Try not to worry, sweetie. You're in good hands. Whenever you start to be afraid, turn your worries into prayers. God's not surprised this is happening. Let's pray that He guides the hands and the minds of the doctors as they make decisions for you and the baby."

Piper nodded. "And will you come with me to Minneapolis?" She couldn't handle the idea of going through this alone.

"I'd be honored, Piper."

Another contraction overcame Piper and she pressed her lips together as the pain twisted her stomach. Mrs. Evans stood beside her, rubbing her back and reassuring her with her words until it passed.

"I'll try getting ahold of Max again," Mrs. Evans said as soon as Piper had recovered from the contraction. "He'll be so upset when he finds out he missed our calls."

Piper couldn't think about Max right now. All she could think about was the baby.

Chapter Fourteen

The two-hour ride to the Twin Cities was the longest ride of Max's life. After he chastised Margo for telling Piper they were a couple, she became angry and refused to talk to him. She was hurt that she'd come all this way thinking he'd fall back at her feet, only to find he wanted nothing to do with her.

"Daddy will *not* be happy with you," Margo said as she pulled up to the players' entrance at the stadium in Minneapolis. "He told me you had a bright career and he could foresee you doing amazing things. He even said he has connections to get you a coaching job, whether at a college or professional level."

"I don't want any of those things, Margo." Max sat in the passenger seat, angry that she finally wanted to talk now, when he was so close to the stadium and his team was inside warming up. "I have no desire to coach college level or professional level football."

"What about the job Daddy offered you?"

Max knew he was blowing his one shot, but he didn't care. There was so much more to life than football. He was ready to do something different with his life. He was happy with the profit he was making at the bed-and-breakfast and wanted to look into other businesses he could invest in. He wanted to give back to Timber Falls and help it grow. He wanted to continue coaching the Timber Falls Lumberjacks, if they'd have him. It was just enough football to satisfy his desire for the game—but not so much it controlled every aspect of his life.

And, more than anything, he wanted to start a life with Piper. His desire to be with her was unlike anything he'd ever experienced. It was a deeper, richer longing than when they were in high school.

"I plan to call your dad and tell him thanks, but I'll have to pass up his offer." Max opened the door and pulled his duffel bag out of the back seat. "I appreciate the effort you took to come here, Margo, but this chapter of my life is closed and I'm ready to start the next one."

Margo let out an angry cry and pressed her foot to the gas pedal. The passenger door slammed shut as she spun out of the stadium lot.

Max was never so happy to see someone walk out of his life.

He jogged to the players' entrance and showed his credentials to the guard at the door. As he walked down the hall, it felt kind of strange to be back at the stadium where his career had ended.

And as he walked onto the field, where the Lumberjacks were warming up, he couldn't have been happier that it was his hometown team who had brought him back to this enormous stadium.

"Coach!" Several players noticed his arrival and it was like a collective sigh of relief passed through them.

"Max." Greg jogged up to Max. "Have you checked your phone?"

"No." It was in his duffel bag. He thought he heard it vibrate a couple times on the drive to the stadium, but he hadn't reached back to check it. "Why?"

"You'll want to call your mom."

Tad was the second person to jog over to Max. He was in his full uniform, but he didn't look ready to play. Fear and uncertainty lined his face. "Something's wrong with Piper and the baby. Mom called me a couple times and said they're airlifting Piper to Abbott Northwestern here in Minneapolis."

Max frowned. "What?" He couldn't seem to make sense of what Tad had said. He just saw Piper two hours ago and everything was fine—how could things change so quickly?

"Call Mom," Tad said. "I talked to her about an hour ago and they were just getting Piper into the medicopter. Something's wrong, but she couldn't talk."

Max dropped his duffel bag and knelt on the ground. He ripped open the zipper and tore through his things, trying to find his phone. His hands shook and his heart raced. What if something happened to Piper or the baby?

He couldn't even think straight as he finally found his phone and turned it on.

He'd missed ten calls from his mom.

The reality of the situation made his stomach turn and he pressed Call, then fumbled to his feet and walked away from the noise of the field.

"Max!" His mom's voice was frantic as she answered the phone. "I'm so relieved that you finally called."

"What's happening?" he asked, breathless. "How are Piper and the baby?"

"We got to Abbott Northwestern about ten minutes ago. They're getting Piper checked in and ready for surgery. The baby isn't stable enough for a regular delivery." Mom was usually the calmest person in a crisis, but her voice cracked and she was crying. "Piper's scared, Max. I wish you were here with her. I can go into the operating room with her, but she needs you."

And Max needed Piper, too. He needed to be there with her, to hold her hand and to reassure her that she wasn't alone. That he would be there for her, no matter what happened.

"I'll be there as soon as I can."

"Hurry. They want to get her into the operating room as soon as possible."

Max ran to a group of stadium employees. "How far is Abbott Northwestern Hospital from here?"

"About a mile," one of them said, a frown on his face. "Does one of the players need a doctor?"

"No." Max shook his head. "My friend was just airlifted there and I need to be by her side."

"I can call an Uber for you," the employee said.

"It'll take too long." Max shook his head. "I'll run."

Tad and Greg had gathered up Max's things and brought them to him. That was when Max remembered why he was at the stadium and his heart fell. "I'm so sorry," he said to Tad.

"Don't worry about it, Max. You need to be with Piper."

"Go," Greg said. "We've got this. Don't worry about us."

"Are you sure?" This was why Max had come back to Timber Falls—to get a championship win for his team.

"This is just the semifinal," Tad said with a shrug. "You won't have any excuse not to be with us in two weeks when we come back here for the championship game. That's the one we'll need you for."

"Are you sure?" he asked again.

"Go!" Tad and Greg said at the same time.

"We can manage without you right now," Tad said. "I don't think Piper can."

It was all he needed to say. Max grabbed his bag and ran.

The employees pointed him in the direction of the hospital down Chicago Avenue.

Max had never run so fast in his life. In less than ten minutes, he entered the Mother Baby Center at Abbott Northwestern Hospital, out of breath, but ready to run as far as it would take.

A nurse was waiting for him at the entrance. "I can tell by the frenzied look on your face that you're Max."

He nodded, his heart pounding harder than it had ever pounded before. "Where's Piper? Can I see her?"

"Your mother told us you'd be coming," she said as she quickly led Max through some double doors into the birthing center. "Here's some hospital scrubs," she said as she handed Max a stack of clothing. "You can put them over your outside clothes." She stopped at a room and nodded toward the door. "You may change in here and then I'll bring you to Mrs. Connelly. She approved your mother to go into the operating room with her, but your mother has assured us Mrs. Connelly will want you there. Of course, we'll check with her before we let you enter the OR."

Max didn't even question her or try to explain as he slipped into a room and put the protective clothing over his athletic gear. He was dressed to coach his football game, but as soon as he put on the hospital garb, he was ready to coach a different team.

"You can keep the mask off until we enter the OR," the nurse said to him from the other side of a curtain. "I'm sure Mrs. Connelly will want to see your face before we head in."

All Max could think about was Piper and the baby. He needed to see her, to touch her, to reassure her—if for no other reason than to reassure himself.

"It'll just be a few more minutes, Mrs. Connelly," a nurse said as she came into the prep room where Piper was waiting. "They're preparing the OR right now."

Piper nodded and forced herself to breathe deeply. She hadn't seen Mrs. Evans since they'd arrived at the hospital, but she'd been reassured that they wouldn't start without her.

Now that all the commotion had eased, and Piper was in the hospital gown, ready to go into surgery, she couldn't think of anything except Max. Where was he? Had he and Margo reconciled?

She forced herself to stop thinking about him as a shiver passed through her. It was so cold, and even though a nurse had brought her a warm blanket, she couldn't stop shivering.

"Right in here, Mr. Evans," a nurse said a moment before Max came around the corner and entered the prep room.

Piper's heart started to pound at the sight of him. She'd never seen anything so wonderful in her life.

He stood in blue hospital scrubs, with a mask hanging on his chest. His brown eyes locked with hers and tears stung the backs of her eyes.

He'd come. He'd left the game and Margo, and he had come.

"Piper." He rushed to her side and pressed a kiss to her lips. "I'm so happy I made it in time."

The tears fell down her cheeks as she received his kiss. Suddenly, she wasn't as afraid to go into the operating room. Having Max by her side made her feel like she could do almost anything. Knowing he'd be there to watch over her and her baby gave her courage. She didn't have to bear this alone.

Her best friend had come to support her.

"I'm so sorry I wasn't there for you, Piper," he said as he knelt by her side.

She shook her head and placed another kiss on his lips. "It's not your fault, Max. I'm just so happy you're here. But what about the game?"

"They can handle things without me. I have a more important team that needs me right now."

She did feel like a team with Max by her side.

"Is this the young fellow who will accompany you into the OR?" a nurse asked Piper.

"Yes." Piper nodded, having no doubt in her mind. There was no one else she'd rather have in the operating room.

"Then let's get you in there." The nurse came to Piper's other side and lifted the handrails on the side of the bed.

Max held Piper's hand and kissed it as he rose to his feet. "May I pray for you?" he asked Piper.

She nodded and closed her eyes as Max said a prayer for her and the baby's safety.

A few minutes later, he walked by her side, holding her hand, as they wheeled her into the operating room.

The bright lights hurt her eyes and another contraction gripped her middle, but it was all bearable with Max close at hand. He whispered soothing words to her and kissed her forehead as the nurses waited for the contraction to pass, and then as the anesthesiologist came in and gave her the medicine needed to perform the cesarean section.

Right behind the anesthesiologist, the doctor she'd met when she'd first arrived came in, dressed in scrubs. His face was covered by his mask, but his eyes were kind as he came to Piper's side.

A sheet had been raised in front of Piper, so she could no longer see her stomach. She was now numb from the waist down as Max stood near her head, still holding her hand. His face was also covered, but his beautiful, loving gaze never left her face.

"Are you ready?" the doctor asked Piper.

She wasn't ready—the baby wasn't ready—but they had little choice. It was best to take the baby now, even if he or she was so early.

"We have a neonatologist in the room, ready to see to your baby the moment we deliver," the doctor said in his reassuring voice. "There is also a team of nurses just for the baby, as well as a team of nurses just for you. We'll have this baby delivered in just a couple minutes."

"Thank you," Piper said.

"My pleasure," the doctor responded and then went back to the other side of the sheet.

The anesthesiologist was close at hand, watching Piper's vital signs, but it felt as if it was just Max and Piper, since she couldn't see anyone beyond the screen.

"Piper," Max said as he bent close to her. "Ever since that day you walked into Vacation Bible School, I've known you could do anything you set your mind to. You've proven to me that you're the bravest, strongest, most courageous woman I've ever known and I'm so proud of you." Tears glistened in his eyes as he spoke to her. "You constantly amaze me."

She was too overcome to respond as the machines beeped and the surgical team worked. His words bolstered her and gave her a sense of confidence she hadn't felt all day.

A few minutes later, a baby cried, and then the doctor's voice came to her through the sheet. "You have a beautiful baby girl, Mrs. Connelly."

A girl. Piper's heart broke, knowing Nick would never meet his little girl—but it also soared, knowing her daughter had finally arrived.

Max looked over the sheet and tears streamed down his face.

Piper couldn't see her daughter, but she could see Max, and if the look on his face meant anything, her daughter was absolutely perfect.

A nurse came to Piper's side and showed her the tiny little bundle, wrapped in the blanket. Piper cried as she kissed her daughter's cheek. She *was* perfect.

"We need to rush her off to the neonatal unit," the nurse said, "but you'll be able to see her as soon as you're out of recovery."

Piper nodded.

"Mr. Evans is welcome to stay with you," the nurse said, "or he may come with the baby."

Max looked to Piper. "Whatever you want," he said.

"Go with her," Piper said. "I don't want her to be alone."

With a gentle smile, Max kissed Piper again, and then he followed the nurse out of the operating room to be with her daughter.

"There goes my heart," Piper whispered to one of the nurses who stayed behind. "My heart and my home."

How would she ever say goodbye to Max now?

Chapter Fifteen

$\sim$

Max felt helpless as he stood in the neonatal intensive care unit and watched Piper's little girl being cared for. The doctor and nurses were efficient as they checked the baby's vitals, gave her oxygen, did a thorough examination, cleaned her and then put a tiny little diaper on her body.

"Five pounds, three ounces," the nurse said as she weighed the baby and glanced at Max. "And eighteen inches long."

"She's so small," Max breathed.

"Would you like to touch her?" the nurse asked.

"May I?"

"Of course. Babies need as much love and attention as possible."

Max was instructed to wash his hands and then rub them together to make sure they were warm. He went to the bed where the baby was lying under the warm light. Her eyes were closed, but she moved her arms.

He took her tiny hand in his and was shocked at how delicate her fingernails were. She squeezed her hand around his finger and his heart clenched in his chest. Tears burned in his eyes and he shook his head. It was hard to believe this was the little blessing pushing against his hand when she was in her mama's tummy just a couple weeks ago.

"Hello," he whispered to the baby, his voice filled with awe.

"She's doing really well," the doctor said to Max when she came up to his side. "Her lungs are nice and strong, which is our biggest concern when they're born under thirty-seven weeks. Her heart is beating at a hundred and thirty beats per minute, nice and steady." She put her hand on Max's arm. "She's perfect. Congratulations."

Max nodded. "Thank you."

"We'll keep her on oxygen for a couple of days and watch her around the clock," the doctor continued. "It's a little early to tell now, but if all continues to go well, she'll probably be able to go home in about two weeks or so."

Max nodded again, uncertain what questions he needed to ask.

"As soon as Mrs. Connelly is out of recovery, she can come in here and meet your daughter properly," the doctor said. "Until then, you're welcome to hold her."

"Me?" Max couldn't imagine holding the baby before Piper—and didn't bother to correct the doctor when she assumed the baby was his.

"The sooner she's held, the better." The doctor nodded at the nurse that the baby was ready to be held.

"Go ahead and have a seat in the rocking chair," the nurse said to Max as she wrapped the baby up in a blanket, making sure her oxygen was still properly attached.

Max took a seat, his hands unsteady and his pulse pounding hard.

Ever so gently, the baby was laid in his arms. Max's heart turned over as he held her. She weighed almost nothing and was so fragile that every instinct he had wanted to protect her.

"Don't be afraid to hold her close and get as much skin-to-skin contact as possible," the nurse said. "Research has found that a baby breathes better, their heart rate is stronger and they spend less time in the NICU when they have contact with their parents."

Again, Max didn't correct her assumption. Instead, he brought the baby up to his face and put her cheek against his own. It was so soft, he could hardly believe it. He kissed her cheek and whispered the most natural thing in the world, coming from the deepest recesses of his heart, "I love you."

Tears gathered in his eyes again as he marveled at this tiny, perfect gift from God.

A couple hours passed as he held the baby with the nurses continuing to see to her needs. Finally, a commotion caused Max to look up.

Piper was being wheeled into the NICU, and when she saw him sitting there, cuddling her daughter, her eyes welled up with tears. He had never loved Piper as much as he did in that moment. He couldn't even explain the feeling to himself, let alone someone else. He'd never felt anything like it in his life.

"Mama's here," Max whispered to the baby.

When Piper was directly in front of Max, he leaned over and passed the baby into her arms.

"Congratulations," a nurse said to Piper. "She's absolutely beautiful."

Piper's eyes shined as she looked down at her daughter. "Thank you."

The nurse left them and went to the other side of the NICU, leaving Piper and Max alone.

"How are you feeling?" Max asked.

"I'm okay for now. The anesthesia hasn't completely worn off yet, but I can feel my feet again." She wiggled her sock-clad toes.

"You were amazing in there," Max said. "*She's* amazing."

"She *is* amazing." Piper brought her up to her lips and kissed her cheek.

"What will you name her?"

"Elaine." Piper ran her finger down her daughter's face, love and awe in her eyes. "Elaine Gwendolyn. Elaine for my mom and Gwendolyn for Nick's mother. But I'll call her Lainey."

"It's beautiful. Nick would be so proud of both of you."

Piper nodded, but didn't respond. It was such a bittersweet moment.

They sat there for a long time, just admiring Lainey.

"Thank you," Piper finally said as she looked up and met Max's gaze. "I'm sorry you had to miss the game."

He hadn't even thought about the game since he'd run through the hospital doors. "I wouldn't want to be anywhere else." He leaned forward and took her free hand in his. He brought it up to his lips and kissed it, his heart expanding in his chest. "For the first time in my life, I ran toward the person I love, and I knew I never wanted to run away again. I love you, Piper, with all my heart and soul." He left his chair and knelt by her side. "I've loved you since the first time I laid eyes on you.

Some people don't think a nine-year-old knows what they want for the rest of their life—but I knew then and I know now." He studied her face. "I want you, I've always wanted you. There's no one else on this planet I want to spend my life with. You're the first thing I want to see when I open my eyes in the morning and the last thing I want to see when I close them at night. I love you passionately, Piper, and if you'll have me, I'll spend the rest of my life showing you how much you mean to me." He put his hand on Lainey's head. It was tiny in comparison. "How much both of you mean to me."

Piper's gaze caressed his face, but there was a sadness in her eyes.

"You don't have to answer me now," Max said quickly. "You've just been through a really tough time and I don't want to make you feel—"

She put her finger up to his lips to quiet him. He took her hand in his and briefly closed his eyes. He loved the feel of her.

"I love you, too, Max," she said quietly. "Having you back in my life means everything to me." She shook her head. "But what about Margo and California, and the opportunities her father has for you?"

"I have no desire to pursue any of that, Piper. I already had all the opportunities I wanted—and I chose to walk away." He put his hand on the side of her face. "I don't want anything but you and Lainey. My life is meaningless without you in it."

"But—what about your career?"

"I'm ready to do something different. I want to start investing in Timber Falls properties and I have a few business ideas I'd like to pursue. If the football team will have me, I'll keep coaching them—but if not, I'm ready for my life to begin, Piper—and it'll begin with you. I really don't care what I do, as long as I do it with you."

She bit her bottom lip as she studied him. "Truly?" she whispered. "You don't want to leave Timber Falls?"

He shook his head.

"You don't want to pursue a career in the football industry?"

"I've had more than my fair share of that industry."

She was quiet for a moment. "Will I be enough for you, Max?"

"Oh, Piper." He leaned forward and put his hands on either side of her face. "You're more than enough— you're my everything." He shook his head. "I'm afraid I won't be worthy of you."

"Max." She smiled through her tears. "I love you. Neither one of us is worthy for the other—but we're perfect for one another."

He leaned in and kissed her. It wasn't a passionate kiss, or even a desperate one. It was sweet and gentle, and full of all the love he held for the woman sitting before him. "Will you marry me?" he asked quietly.

She didn't hesitate. "Yes."

His heart soared and he was afraid he was dreaming. At long last, Piper would become his wife.

The nurse returned to them, a smile on her lips. "Can I take your family's first picture?"

"Would you?" Max asked. He took his cell phone out of his back pocket and saw that he'd missed dozens of texts.

A grin split his face. "It looks like the Lumberjacks are going on to the championship game," he said to Piper.

Piper smiled with Max. "Congratulations."

As Max put his arm around Piper, and smiled at the nurse as she took their picture, he knew he didn't deserve the blessings God was lavishing on him—but he would spend the rest of his life giving thanks.

The two weeks at the hospital went by faster than Piper had expected. She was released after two days, but she was able to sleep in Lainey's room in the infant care center at the Mother Baby Center. Those days with her baby were the sweetest times in her life, especially because Max was there as often as possible, and several friends came to visit, including Max's mom who treated Lainey like the granddaughter she would soon become when Max and Piper were married.

Max drove just under the speed limit all the way back to Timber Falls as Lainey slept in her car seat. Piper sat in the back seat with their daughter, but several times on the two-hour ride, Max reached back and took her hand, smiling at her in the rearview mirror.

"Are you certain you want to do this?" he asked her as they pulled into the Timber Falls Community Church parking lot just as the sun set. "Don't you want to wait for a big church wedding, with all the trappings you usually plan for brides? Will you feel cheated?"

Piper shook her head, more certain than ever before. "I've planned more weddings than you can imagine, and they all have one thing in common, the most important thing—at the end of the day, two people are married. All that matters to me is that when you and I bring Lainey home, she has a mom and a dad—and you and I are husband and wife." She reached toward him and he took her hand. "I love you, Max. Nothing else matters."

"If you change your mind," he said, "and you want a big party to celebrate later on, don't hesitate to tell me."

"What about you?" she asked. "Wouldn't you rather be in Minneapolis with your team tonight, getting ready for the big game tomorrow?"

He glanced at her in the rearview mirror and simply smiled. "You know I wouldn't."

A recent addition had been added to the back of the church where the new school was housed, so they had to park in the new parking lot on the west side of the building.

Max came to the back door and opened it for Piper. She stepped out and he reached in to gently remove Lainey, his careful movements making Piper smile. He put her diaper bag on his shoulder and carried Lainey in the crook of his arm, while using his free hand to take Piper's.

Piper felt amazing being two weeks postpartum. Her incision was healing well and nothing hurt anymore. With all the help from the hospital staff, she felt surprisingly rested. She was even able to fit back into some of her pre-pregnancy clothes, though she was still wearing loose-fitting things that didn't rub on her incision.

"Liv said she'd take care of all the details," Piper said to Max as they walked toward the church. "I have no idea what she pulled together, but I do know we'll be surrounded by all of our friends. What more could we ask for?"

Max let go of Piper's hand and opened the door for her, then he followed her inside with Lainey.

Liv was waiting in the vestibule near the door, a grin on her face. "What took you two so long?"

Piper glanced at Max and he didn't look even a little embarrassed by his excessively careful driving.

"We stopped about a half an hour ago so I could feed Lainey," Piper said. "It took a little longer than I expected, but she should be content for another hour or two."

"Your mom is waiting in the nursery to take care of Lainey while the two of you get ready," Liv said to Max. "Tad will tell you what to do. We'll meet you in the sanctuary in about half an hour."

Max leaned forward and placed a gentle kiss on Piper's lips. "The next time I kiss you, you'll be Piper Evans."

"At last," she said.

He walked away from her, with Lainey in his arms, and she couldn't help but smile, getting a little teary-eyed.

Liv gave Piper a big hug and then said, "Okay, enough with all that. You have a wedding to attend!"

Piper followed her friend to one of the new restrooms on the main floor of the church. When Liv opened the door, Piper put her hands up to cover her mouth.

There, hanging from a hook, was an elegant white gown. It had an empire-style waist, so it wouldn't be formfitting. The skirt was long, as were the sleeves. It was beautiful, yet simple—and exactly what Piper would have chosen for herself.

"Oh, Liv!" Piper said. "When I asked you to grab one of my gowns from my closet, I didn't think you'd go out and buy a new one!"

"Every bride should have a special gown for her

wedding day." She smiled and her eyes twinkled with mischief. "Prepare to be pampered—if only for a little while."

There was a knock at the door and Piper's hairdresser came in. "We don't have much time," she said. "But I know just what to do with your beautiful hair."

"And I'm doing your makeup," Liv said, rubbing her hands together. "Let's get started. We need to get you to that sanctuary in thirty minutes or your groom will come looking for you."

Piper pressed her lips together, trying not to cry. "Thank you," she said.

Liv winked. "You're welcome. You deserve the best, Piper."

Thirty minutes later, Piper left the ladies' room feeling like a completely different woman—and definitely not a woman who gave birth to her first child just thirteen days ago.

Liv wore a pretty soft-pink gown, since Piper had asked her to be her maid of honor. Tad would serve as Max's best man and Piper planned to walk down the aisle by herself.

When they got to the lobby just outside the sanctuary, two gorgeous bouquets of soft-pink roses were waiting. One for Piper and one for Liv.

"You thought of everything, didn't you?" Piper asked Liv.

"I hope so," Liv said as she moved one of Piper's curls over her shoulder. "If not, I'm not very good at my job, am I?"

Liv stepped in front of Piper and knocked on the doors, which were opened from within.

The music shifted from *Canon in D* to Mendelssohn's "Wedding March." Piper stared in amazement as the congregation rose to their feet.

It was no small wedding, by any stretch of the imagination. Friends, neighbors, church family and Max's entire football team, including their parents, were waiting in the sanctuary. They weren't in Minneapolis, after all.

They had come to support their coach.

Max stood at the front of the sanctuary in the suit he'd worn to the homecoming dance, his hair combed and his beard freshly trimmed. His eyes glowed when he saw Piper and she felt like the most beautiful woman in the whole world. He didn't look at anyone other than her as she walked down the aisle to join him.

Mrs. Evans sat in the front row with Lainey in her arms, tears sliding down her face as she smiled at Piper.

Pastor Jacob Dawson and Tad stood near Max, and when Piper finally arrived at the altar, her legs weak and her hands trembling with joy, Max took her hand in his and drew her to his side as if he had no intention of ever letting her go.

And perhaps, he didn't.

"We are gathered here today to celebrate with Piper and Max as they proclaim their love and commitment to the world," Pastor Jacob said with a smile. "We are gathered to rejoice, with and for them, in the new life they now undertake together. Let us pray."

The ceremony went by in a blur, but after she and Max declared their intention to wed, and said their vows and slipped gold bands on each other's fingers, Pastor Jacob declared that they were husband and wife.

"What God has brought together," the pastor said, "let no man separate. You may kiss your bride, Max."

Max put his hands on either side of Piper's face and gently kissed her.

Piper felt the kiss all the way to the tips of her toes and out to the ends of her fingertips. Her body hummed with the joy his touch gave her and she responded by wrapping her arms around his neck to pull him closer. The congregation cheered and they pulled apart, Piper's cheeks aflame with embarrassment.

As the pianist played a recessional, Max took Piper by the hand and led her to his mother where he took Lainey from her and cradled her in his arm.

"This is what God has brought together," he said to Piper. "From this day forward."

They walked out of the sanctuary and stood in the lobby, waiting for their guests to come out and greet them, but before they did, Max leaned over and whispered in her ear, "The night before my high school championship game, I made the biggest mistake of my life and lost you. I'm so happy that the night before this championship game, I made the best decision of my life and now you're mine forever."

Pleasure filled Piper's heart and she stood on tiptoe to kiss her husband.

Forever didn't seem long enough.

Chapter Sixteen

Max stood on the sidelines at the Vikings' stadium, his heart pounding as he watched the last play in the Timber Falls Lumberjacks' championship game. There were thirteen seconds left in the final quarter and the Lumberjacks had possession of the ball. The score was twenty-four to twenty-eight and they were only five yards shy of the goal—and the win.

As Tad broke up the huddle and the offensive line got into position, Max held his breath. Several scouts were in the audience, watching Tad's every move—but it hadn't seemed to phase Tad. If anything, his brother was playing the best game of his life.

From where Max stood, he couldn't hear his brother give the call, but the team went into motion and Tad dropped back, his hand on the ball as he scanned left and then right, and then threw the ball to his buddy, Aiken Hendrickson, their wide receiver. Aiken was right where he was supposed to be and the ball sailed through the air, past several players and landed in Aiken's hands, as if there was no one else on the field.

A roar went up from the crowd as the clock ran out

and the refs threw their hands up, indicating a successful goal.

Max yelled and jumped, energy and adrenaline coursing through his body. Everyone rushed the field and lifted Tad and Aiken onto their shoulders.

Up in the stands, Max's mom was waving and cheering and clapping, and Max could almost imagine seeing his dad sitting next to her, a grin on his face.

The only thing that would make this moment perfect was if Piper and Lainey could be there, but he had to take solace knowing they were back in Timber Falls watching the livestream, cheering and clapping along with everyone else from town.

Max had finally redeemed his past mistakes and given Timber Falls a championship title, in the very same stadium where he'd played his last game in the NFL.

As Max lifted his hands toward heaven to praise God, he was also lifted onto the shoulders of his team and he met Tad's happy gaze. They were brought together and Max gave his little brother a hug.

"Good job, Tad," Max said over the noise.

"Thanks for coming home to coach us, Max," Tad said. "We couldn't have done it without you."

The crowd started to chant Max's name and when he was put back on the ground, he went to shake hands with the coach from the other team. After that, the organizers of the Minnesota High School League set up the awards on the field. When everyone finally calmed down, they made a formal presentation to the Timber Falls Lumberjacks and handed the large trophy to Max.

For as long as he lived, he would hold three memories close to his heart. The day he married Piper, the day he held Lainey for the first time and the day he brought home a trophy for the Lumberjacks.

He could hardly believe that all three had taken place in a two-week time frame.

But, what made him truly happy was that when all the chaos and noise and celebration came to an end, the most exciting part of his day would just get started. He would go home to Piper and Lainey.

It was late, but Piper was still awake. The third-floor apartment where she and Max had brought Lainey home just the day before was cozy as Piper sat on the sofa, Lainey in her arms.

No matter how much she gazed at her baby, she could never get enough of her. Lainey had already filled out so much in the two weeks since her birth. She had put on almost a pound of weight, bringing her up to six pounds. She was still a little squirt, but she was healthy and beautiful.

A cup of hot chocolate sat on the coffee table by Piper as she softly sang to Lainey. Mrs. Anderson had been up earlier to bring Piper supper and to watch the championship game, but when the trophy had been handed to Max, and they had finished cheering and crying, Mrs. Anderson had taken the dirty dishes back downstairs, where she had probably put them in the dishwasher and then gone to bed.

The house was full with guests, but up here, tucked into the third floor, Piper felt all alone with her baby girl as they waited for Max to come home.

A creak at the back door made Piper's heart skip a beat in anticipation, and a moment later, Max was there, a grin on his face as he quietly walked across the living room and set the large, championship trophy on a side table before he bent over the back of the couch to give Piper a kiss.

"Congratulations," she said. "It was an amazing game. I'm so proud of you."

His smile only grew brighter. "I've never been happier about a football game in my life. But winning the championship dimmed in comparison to the knowledge that I was coming home to you and Lainey. I haven't stopped smiling since yesterday." Max came around the couch and sat beside his wife. "I'm a little worried that I won't ever be able to wipe this grin off my face and I'll drive everyone crazy whenever they look at me."

Piper's own smile had been a permanent fixture since yesterday, as well. "I know what you mean."

Max kissed the top of Lainey's head and she wiggled in Piper's arms.

"How has she been?" he asked.

"A little fussy earlier today, but really good, other than that."

"Can I take her?" he asked.

She nodded and handed Lainey over to her daddy.

Max held her in his big hands and she fit perfectly.

Piper watched them, her heart feeling like it might explode with love. After a little while, she got up and went to the desk in the kitchen. "Liv stopped by today and dropped this off."

She showed the piece of paper to Max. It was a check from the Custer wedding—and it was just enough to pay off the last of Nick's debt. "I'm putting it in the bank tomorrow and then I'm paying off the last bit of debt I owe." She sat next to Max again and looked at the check in her hands. "I feel like God is offering us a fresh start." She leaned on his shoulder and he rested his head on hers. "While you were gone today, I had a really good heart-to-heart with God. It was time for me to let go of the past—all of it. I've finally forgiven my parents and Nick, and I'm ready to move on."

Max kissed the top of her head. "I'm proud of you, Piper."

"I know old habits die hard and it'll be a conscious decision to forgive them each time a bad memory comes up, but I know in time, the pain will heal, and I hope that one day, when I think about them, I don't just remember the bad times. I want to remember the good times, too. And I want to think about all the positive things that came from those hard situations."

"Like this little girl right here," Max said as he lifted Lainey and placed a kiss on her forehead.

Piper touched her daughter's soft cheek. "What the enemy intended for evil," she whispered, "God has used for good."

"'Every good and perfect gift is from above,'" Max quoted from the Book of James, "'coming down from the Father of the heavenly lights.'"

"We should have that engraved and hang it above the door," Piper said, "so that every day, we can be reminded that God is in the business of giving His children gifts."

Max kissed Piper then, and she savored the touch, allowing him to deepen the kiss until she was breathless.

"It's been a long day," he said, "and this little one won't let us sleep for long." He stood and offered Piper his free hand, then they went into Lainey's nursery and laid her in her bed.

They stood by her crib for a long time, Max's arms encircling Piper as they looked down at their child.

She thought back to the day Max had arrived in Timber Falls, and she recalled the vast array of emotions that had filled her heart. Anger. Heartbreak. Disappointment.

Hope.

At the time, she'd been afraid of that final one—of hope, because she knew if her heart was broken again, she wouldn't be able to bear up under it. But God had a different plan—not one of heartbreak, but one of redemption and healing.

Max Evans was finally home and all was as it should be.

* * * * *

If you liked this story from Gabrielle Meyer,
check out her previous Love Inspired books:

A Mother's Secret
Unexpected Christmas Joy

Available now from Love Inspired!
Find more great reads at www.LoveInspired.com.

Dear Reader,

When I wrote *A Home for Her Baby*, I used the Waller House Inn, my favorite bed-and-breakfast, as inspiration for the Warren House Bed & Breakfast. Sadly, soon after this story was completed, the COVID pandemic spread across this planet and not one single town was spared its devastating effects. Thankfully, at the time of this writing, our small town has had few cases, but it has had an economic impact that I'm sure we'll feel for years to come. Unfortunately, my friends at the Waller House Inn were forced to close their beautiful doors for good. I dedicated this book to my daughter, but I would like to offer an honorary dedication to Scott and Raquel Lundberg, owners of the Waller House Inn, for their amazing hospitality and dedication to our community. God's blessings on the next leg of your journey.

Gabrielle Meyer

SPECIAL EXCERPT FROM

LOVE INSPIRED
INSPIRATIONAL ROMANCE

*Running a small Amish coffee shop is all Lydia Stoltzfus
needs to be satisfied with her life—until her next-door
neighbor and childhood crush, Simon Fisher, returns
home with his five-year-old daughter. Now, even as
she falls for the shy little girl, Lydia must resist her
growing feelings for Simon...*

*Read on for a sneak preview of
A Secret Amish Crush by Marta Perry.
Available March 2021 from Love Inspired.*

"You want me to say you were right about Aunt Bess
and the matchmaking, don't you? Okay, you were right,"
Simon said.

"I thought you'd come to see it my way," Lydia said
lightly. "It didn't take your aunt long to get started, did
it?"

His only answer was a growled one. "You wouldn't
understand."

"Look, I do see what the problem is," she said. "You
don't want people to start thinking that you're tied up
with me when you have someone else in mind."

"I don't have anyone in mind." Simon sounded as if
he'd reached the end of his limited patience. "I'm not
going to marry again—not you, not anyone. I found love
once, and I don't suppose anyone has a second chance at
a love like that."

LIEXP0221

His bleak expression wrenched her heart, and she couldn't find any response.

He frowned, staring at the table as if he were thinking of something. "What do you suppose would happen if I hinted to Aunt Bess that I was thinking that way, but that I really needed to get to know you without scaring you off?"

"I don't know. She might be even worse. Still, I guess you could try it."

"Not just me," he said. "You'd have to at least act as if you were willing to be friends."

Somehow she had the feeling that she'd end up regretting this. But on the other hand, he could hardly discourage her from trying to help Becky in that case.

"Just one thing. If we're supposed to be becoming friends, then you won't be angry if I take an interest in Becky now, will you?"

He nodded. "All right. But…" He seemed to grow more serious. "If this makes you uncomfortable for any reason, we stop."

She tried to chase away the little voice in her mind that said she'd get hurt if she got too close to him. "No problem," she said firmly, and slammed the door on her doubts.

Don't miss
A Secret Amish Crush
by Marta Perry, available wherever
Love Inspired books and ebooks are sold.

LoveInspired.com

LOVE INSPIRED
INSPIRATIONAL ROMANCE

UPLIFTING STORIES OF FAITH, FORGIVENESS AND HOPE.

Join our social communities to connect with other readers who share your love!

Sign up for the Love Inspired newsletter at **LoveInspired.com** to be the first to find out about upcoming titles, special promotions and exclusive content.

HARLEQUIN

Heartfelt or thrilling, passionate or uplifting—Harlequin is more than just happily-ever-after.

With twelve different series to choose from and new books available every month, you are sure to find stories that will move you, uplift you, inspire and delight you.

HNEWS2021